DIVER'S DAUGHTER

PATRICE LAWRENCE

Series Consultant:
Tony Bradman

■SCHOLASTIC

THE FIRST DIVE

I hit the water. No, it hit me. It slapped me in the face then pulled me under. My head filled with its stink. I tried to hold my breath, but the water's wet fingers were in my nostrils, inching up and up. I couldn't open my mouth to scream; if I did, I'd be dead. But at this rate, I was going to be dead anyway. The River Thames's strong arms yanked me, away from the boat, away from my mother, away from my life.

Below the surface, the Thames talks to you. It's the stab of beaks as the gulls dive for fish. It's the sound of oars plunging in and out of the heavy water as pilots guide the merchant ships up to Wool Quay. As I sank further down, I thought I heard different sounds, proper voices, children's voices like mine. If I could open my eyes, I was sure I'd see those children floating on the current, children like me who'd wobbled and fallen.

"Tell us your story, Eve," they whispered. "Tell us your story."

A POPPET FOR A PENNY

My name is Eve. I'm twelve years old and I'm surprised I've lived that long. I'm a Southwark girl, born and bred – just outside London across the River Thames – but I've lived in other places too.

Sometimes I still wake up in the middle of the night gasping for breath. In my dreams, the bed linen turns to water, pressing against my eyes, blocking my ears to everything apart from my slamming heart. Then I hear my mother calling.

"*Mpendwa*, you are safe."

She calls me *mpendwa*, her beloved. I surface out of my nightmare into the morning.

Three times I've ended up in deep water, so far. Twice I nearly drowned. The third time – well, I'm getting ahead of myself. I'll start by telling you about the first time.

It was the last day of the Bartholomew Fair. I'd never been to the fair before, even though every year

Mama had promised to take me. You know what adults are like. They look you in the eye, make you a promise and then forget it by the time they look away. But Mama isn't like that. She doesn't make promises that she doesn't think she can keep, because so many people have broken promises to her.

There was a good reason why Mama hadn't kept her promise before. The fair lasts for three days in August and on the first day, every year, I'd wake up, lie still and listen. Every year, I'd hear the same thing: rain. I could hear it dripping into the pots Mama had lined up under the eaves. That is, the years when we even had eaves, of course. The August before, we'd had nowhere to sleep and we came close to being arrested as vagabonds. Eventually we'd sneaked into a grain store, but we spent the dark hours fighting what must have been the King Rat of Southwark. I knew that we definitely wouldn't be going to the fair that year.

The summers when we did have somewhere to live, I'd creep out of bed and check outside to see how bad the rain was and it would always be the same. Mud and dung oozing across the cobbles, trampled into a slippery mix by horses' hooves, with little rivers of mud running along the pathways, mixing the muck into a special sticky mess that never wanted to let go of you. Even the dogs looked sideways at it and tried to find a way round it. Mama and I didn't have fancy leather boots or even a pair of clogs to get us through that mess. I just had my old pumps and no matter how many times Mama tried to sew it back, the seam kept unravelling, so my toe stuck out the front. By the time I'd walked three steps in that mud, I'd have been barefoot.

Even if we had braved it on the muddy streets, we would still have had to cross the river to get to London. The quickest way was by wherry boat, as the bridge was always jammed with carts and traders. But who wanted to sit in a small boat on a wild, deep river in the rain? So every year, instead of going to the fair, I ended up doing chores. Last year, I churned butter from dawn to dinner. After that, my arms were so strong I could have squeezed the butter straight from the cow.

This day was different. We'd been lodging at the Boar's Head, an inn off Tooley Street, up under the eaves again. I woke while it was still dark. Mama had left buckets out, but I couldn't hear the *drop, drop* of water. I squinted into the darkness. I could just about see the dark shapes of the dresser and Mama's sewing basket on the table. The travellers in the room below were laughing and singing and someone in another room was coughing hard. I could hear the ostler, who looked after the guests' horses, humming to himself in the courtyard and then the clop of the horses' hooves as he led them to the stables. Next to me, Mama was still sleeping so I knew it must be very early in the morning. I didn't want to leave my warm place in the bed because it had taken me a long time to get comfortable last night. The inn had been busy and Master Horstead, the landlord, had Mama serving guests long into the night. It was hard for me to sleep when Mama wasn't next to me. It still is.

I had turned on to my side to try to go back to sleep, but something was wrong. No, something was right! I'd gone to sleep listening to the rain falling into the buckets, but it was all quiet now. I lay perfectly still and listened. No rain. I nudged Mama.

"Go back to sleep, Eve."

I sat up, pulling the blanket from her. She tried to yank it back, but I was holding it tight.

"Listen, Mama! The rain's stopped!"

"What if it has?" she grumbled.

"It means we can go the fair!"

I scrambled out of bed and looked out of the window. A faint line of light spread up from the east. A dog barked and it started all the others barking too. Mistress Sleet opened her window and shouted at them. She should have known better. The dogs just thought she meant "bark louder".

Mama sighed and sat up. "Are you sure it's not raining?"

"Yes! We can go, can't we?"

"We'll see, *mpendwa*."

Mama's "we'll see" could mean "yes", but I had to be patient. It wasn't just down to her to decide. Master Horstead usually had a long list of chores for Mama to do and then Mistress Horstead had an even longer one on top of that. Mama had to do them. If she didn't, they'd make us pay more for our room, and we couldn't afford that. We didn't want to end up fighting rats in the grain store again. We knew we were lucky that we even had this. So, Mama set off to change the bed linen in the rooms that had been occupied while I cleaned the chimney grates and built up the kindling and wood ready for fresh fires. After that, we went down to help prepare the day's food. Then we waited and waited. Finally Mistress Horstead gave us permission to go to the fair, so long as we returned in time to help serve the guests in the evening.

At last! I was really going to the famous Bartholomew Fair! First though, we had to get there. On fair days the bridge across to London was more crowded than ever. I thought we would at least try, but Mama said no. By the time we'd managed to get across to the other side, she said, we'd have to turn around and come right home again. I'm sure she was right and that was one of her reasons for saying no, but I also knew that there was something on the bridge that she didn't want to see: the traitors – or what was left of them.

You see, I was born in 1558, the same year that Queen Elizabeth became queen. Mama hadn't been in England very long, so didn't really know what life had been like here before, but the old people in the taverns still talked about it. It had been a hard time for everyone. The Portuguese on the island where Mama was born were Catholics, like England had been, but when Elizabeth became queen, England didn't know what it wanted. Queen Elizabeth's father, King Henry VIII, had been Catholic, but then he'd stopped and made himself head of a new Church of England so that he could marry Elizabeth's mother. When he changed his religion, everyone else was meant to as well. When Henry died, his son Edward didn't change things, but Edward died when he wasn't much older than me. Then his Catholic sister, Mary, became queen and everyone was supposed to be Catholic again. I'd heard that she'd wanted to kill everyone who wasn't a Catholic. Now it was Elizabeth who was queen and it was forbidden to be Catholic again.

It didn't bother me so much as nobody had bothered asking Mama and me how we worshipped. But Queen

Elizabeth had upset many people who had thought they could be Catholic again. The ones that were caught found themselves locked up in the Tower of London. Once they'd confessed to being Catholic, their heads were chopped off and stuck on pikes on top of the gateway to the bridge as a warning to others. You couldn't see their faces because they were covered in tar, but Mama still thought their eyes were watching her.

So, no going over the bridge. That meant crossing in a wherry boat. I was nervous, but reminded myself that this was part of the big adventure. As we walked towards the river stairs on Pepper Alley, we soon realized that we weren't the only ones with that plan. The whole of Southwark seemed to be heading to the fair, jostling on the jetty for a boat to take them across the water. The tide was low. It looked like we could almost walk across the stones and mud to London, but even like this, the water could be deadly. Mama held me tightly. People sometimes look at us because our skin is browner than everyone else's, and Mama always worried that something might happen to us. I think that was because of what had happened to her in the past.

At last we reached the front of the queue for the boats. I couldn't help smiling. The sky was bright blue and tiny clouds looked like smudged fingerprints. A gull dipped down into the water and flapped away with a fish in its beak. I held Mama's hand tighter and she smiled down at me. Even the wherrymen were smiling. Of course, fair days were their favourite. They would have a heavy purse of money by the end.

We found ourselves sharing a boat with a farmer and a live goose. The goose was in a basket, but was far from happy about it and showed its displeasure by trying to peck the farmer through the reeds. I could feel the river's strength beneath our little boat as the wherryman weaved between the other vessels. I counted eight more wherries heading back to Southwark. Through the bridge's arches, I glimpsed a galleon, a huge sailing ship, anchored at the wharf on the other side of the river. I asked Mama where she thought it had come from, but she didn't reply. As we came close to shore, a barge cut across us, gliding towards Westminster. The goose flapped around and the boat rocked harder, making the wherryman swear. Mama cuddled me in to her and didn't let go until we safely reached the other side.

We scrambled out on to Puddle Dock and for a little while afterwards I was still swaying, though I could have just been dizzy with excitement. We joined the noisy crowds heading up the narrow streets towards the fair. We heard it before we saw it. A trumpet, street criers and the shouts of laughter became louder as we drew nearer. Soon I could smell the fair too, wafts of roasting

10

meat curling their way over us. I imagined whole pigs and lambs turning on spits, sausages and hams and all the fruit that Mama had told me about. Apricots and oranges – fruit I never even dreamed that I'd taste.

Boom! Boom! Boom! As we came on to Smithfield, a girl marched towards us banging a drum. She was about the same age as me, a little taller, with a cloud of light-brown hair that her bonnet couldn't hold in. She was wearing a white gown with blue stars sewn on to the skirt, and every time the drumstick thumped down, her bonnet gave a little shake, threatening to fly free. She stopped in front of us, drumstick in the air, and gave Mama a little bow.

"Good mistress," said the girl. "Do you care to know the secret to your fortune? Do you wish to know how the stars fall for you and your daughter? Do your humours feel out of balance on this fine, beautiful day?"

Before Mama could reply, the girl leaned towards us, like she was telling us a secret.

"My brother, Griffin, is the best soothsayer in the whole fair. He learned from the Queen's own favourite, the great John Dee himself. You will find us next to the fire-eater."

I tugged Mama's hand. "Can we have our stars read?"

Mama smiled. "Be patient, Eve! There are so many things to see."

She was right. Over in one corner, the sharps had set up tables for games of shove ha'penny and dice, offering a heavy purse to anyone who could beat them. I laughed. I recognized two of the rogues from the ale houses in Southwark. The gamblers who didn't lose their money at the tables would lose it to the pickpockets watching carefully nearby.

An acrobat had slung a rope between two poles, higher than our heads. He stood on it, one foot stretched out, carefully finding its place before the other foot lifted, all while carrying a shrieking woman on his back. We wriggled our way through the shouting crowd. In a clearing, two men were dodging and smashing sticks together, their faces shiny with sweat. One had a bleeding cut above his eyebrow. I wanted to stay and watch, but Mama pulled me away.

"Are you hungry?" she asked me.

I was always hungry! She knew that. She showed me a handful of coins.

"I've been saving these for this very day!"

We were richer than I expected. I wondered if Mama had carefully put aside a little money on all the years that it had been raining too hard for us to come. We walked past trays of fat, dark figs and pale-green plums, cauldrons of pottage and tables groaning with cheeses, tubs of pickled herrings and pies. But I knew what I wanted and I led Mama back to the hog roast, watching carefully as the stallholder carved the slices for us. We found a patch of grass and settled down to enjoy our food. As I sunk my teeth into the soft, smoky meat, I wondered what it would be like to eat this every day. It wouldn't have to be pork. Mutton would do, or capons roasted with herbs or... I sighed. It would *never* happen. Maybe that was a good thing because if it did, I wouldn't appreciate it as much as I was enjoying this now.

Afterwards, we walked around again. I saw the drummer girl. She raised her eyebrows at us, but Mama shook her head. She'd decided it was time to go. The sky to the east was starting to darken, and Mistress Horstead would be expecting us. There was also too much ale being swilled and that always leads to fights. We wanted to be out of the way before the brawling started. We wormed our way through the crowds, back towards the edges of the fair, and then a stall caught my eye. The woman behind it had a pale, lined face and a wide, friendly smile that made her eyes crinkle up.

On the table in front of her were row after row of poppets. Some looked floppy, made from rags and wool, with faces stitched from dark thread. Mama had made me one like that when I was little, but I had lost it on our travels. Others were wooden with carved faces and gowns made from rich fabrics. The woman held up one of the smaller poppets and beckoned me. Before Mama could grab me, I ran towards it.

"Do you like it?" the woman asked.

I reached out to touch it, but she shook her head. It had a wooden head, the colour of my skin. Its body was softer, made from fabric, dressed in a blue gown topped with a crisp white apron. Dark hair poked out from beneath its bonnet.

"It will bring you luck," the woman said.

"We need luck, don't we, Mama?" I said.

"Yes." Mama laughed quietly. "We do, but I'm not sure a poppet is the way to find it. You are far too old for toys, Eve."

The lady nodded, like she understood. "It's not just a poppet. It's a lucky poppet, so lucky I can sell it cheap. Just three halfpence. That's all it costs to buy you luck."

Mama shook her head. "I could buy a whole chicken for that."

The woman frowned, then sighed. "A scrawny chicken will give you a couple of mouthfuls of chewy meat. This poppet will bring you and your daughter good luck for the rest of your long lives. I will take one penny for it, even though that will break me." She gave me a sad smile. "I want you to have all the luck, young sweetheart."

I stayed quiet. I was from Southwark. I knew all the tricks.

Mama handed over the penny and the woman passed me the doll. I smiled at her, but she was already hailing new customers. I clutched the poppet to me as we trotted back towards the river. A wind had struck up and it felt like it would bring rain with it.

"We'll take the bridge," Mama said.

The tide was high by now. As we approached the river, we could see the wherrymen having to work harder to ferry their passengers from shore to shore. Mama looked up at the darkening sky, then down at the water churning through the piers under the bridge. Downstream even the cargo boats seemed to be trying to shake free from their moorings.

The bridge, though, was truly blocked. A horse had collapsed, tipping over its cart full of barrels. Black, tar-like pitch spilled across the cobbles. Crowds were shouting and trying to push past, without walking in the sticky mess. We tried to find a gap to pass through, but it was impossible. The people heading to London wanted to reach it before the city gates were locked for the night, while those leaving were intent on arriving safely in Southwark while there was light. There are many desperate rogues on our side of the river and few watchmen to stop them.

"The wherry it is," Mama said. "Let's be quick before the weather worsens."

This time there was even more of a jostle for boats. As well as people like us returning home, young men and women were looking to enjoy the theatres and beast-baiting on Bankside. Many of them looked like they'd already been enjoying the ale houses around the fair. Mama used her shoulder to get us to the front, but refused to take the first boat. She said the wherryman looked drunk. The tide was at its highest. We needed steady hands.

A man shoved Mama aside. "Move if you're not travelling."

He was tall and I could smell the beer on his breath. It was hard to see his face properly in the twilight. Judging by his clothes, he was far away from being a gentleman.

Mama drew herself up. "I can assure you, sir, we are travelling."

The man looked Mama up and down. She stared back.

The man nodded. "Please accept my apologies." He took his purse from his pocket and drew out a handful of coins. "Allow me to pay for your passage."

He stepped into the wobbling boat and passed the money to the wherryman.

The wherryman studied the coins. "Where to?"

Mama looked from the man to the coins. Was she going to refuse? Mama was always suspicious of strangers.

"Tell him where you want to go," the man instructed. "The fare is paid."

"To the church stairs, please," Mama said.

Mama stepped into the boat and held out her hand to help me in. The boat only had two seats so I settled myself on Mama's lap. The man who had paid our fare took the other seat. She sat upright, gripping me with one hand and the side of the boat with the other. I felt her flinch every time the boat lurched on the tide.

The boat pushed off and the wherryman set to with his oars. We'd only just left the quay when it felt like the river had reached up, grasped the hull of our boat and was tugging it downstream towards the bridge. Mama gripped me harder as water splashed over us. The other passenger had closed his eyes and was moving his mouth like he was praying. I held my poppet to my chest. *If you really are lucky, now is the time to show it.*

The wherryman laughed. "Old Father Thames is having a dance tonight."

"God have mercy!"

The shout came from beside me. The man next to

us was sitting upright, eyes staring ahead.

"Starboard! Ahoy!"

Another wherry swerved towards us. I glimpsed the passengers' terrified faces before it veered away. Our wherryman swore and rowed harder. I knew that if I looked to my left, I'd see the arches beneath the bridge; I could already hear the water gushing through. If your boat was caught in that stream, it was like a monster took hold of you. You were thrown in the air before being sent in to the spinning depths.

We were in the middle of the river now, the rain a slow, steady drizzle that soaked my clothes.

"Stop, boatman! Turn back!" The man was struggling to his feet.

"Please," Mama said. "Stay seated."

Her voice was whipped away by the wind. The wherryman shouted something cruder, but the man ignored him.

"Turn back!" the man shouted. "Before you kill us all!"

"Sit down, sir!" Mama held on to me and tried to grab his arm at the same time. The boat lurched and more water slopped over the side. Mama's nails were digging into my stomach. I tried to breathe, but my chest felt as if it had been hammered so flat, my breathing couldn't work.

"Return, boatman! Return!" The man lunged towards the wherryman to seize the oar from him.

The boat shook as the wherryman fought him off.

"Stop!" Mama let me go to try and force the men apart.

The boat twisted towards the bridge. Suddenly, I saw not only the arches, but every brick and every crack between every brick. I heard the splash and howl of the water as it shot between the pillars. Then the boat pitched and I hit the water.

No, it hit me.

THE CARPENTER'S TALE

Time stopped. As the river reached up from its bed to drag me down, I heard the children asking me to tell them my story. Suddenly, an arm as tight as a belt circled my waist and drew me upwards. It was an angel, I was sure. Mama said I had been baptized, so when I opened my eyes, I knew I would be in Heaven.

I broke the surface of the river. I coughed. The roast pork and river water shifted in my stomach. I wanted to open my eyes and move my arms and legs, but the river had made me heavy. Water swilled in and out of my ears. I could hear the heavy, dull thud of my heart, then came the sound of watermen calling for trade and the rush of the tide. I stopped moving. I hadn't thought that Heaven would sound like Southwark.

"Eve?" Was that Mama's voice?

Then a man. "Pass her up!"

Strong hands on my waist lifted me and other hands grabbed my wrists and heaved. The wind bit through my wet clothes and my face and arms prickled with the chill. My knees knocked something hard and the pain made me open my eyes. The world was a blur. They laid me across cold, wet wood and I curled myself into a ball.

"She's alive!"

That wasn't Mama. I wanted her. I didn't care if we were in Heaven or still on Earth, but I wanted Mama now.

"Help me." *That* was Mama.

My floppy neck wouldn't let me turn to see her. My heavy arms wouldn't let me help her. I heard a scrambling and the boat rolled to the side. I tumbled off the bench and into a pool of water at the bottom of the boat.

"Mama?" My voice was too weak to come out of my mouth.

"Eve? *Mpendwa*, I'm here."

A stub of candle glowed on the dresser. I breathed in its meaty tallow smell. I was in bed, Mama's and my bed. I recognized the dip of the mattress. Even if Mama and I started off at opposite edges of the bed, we always ended up cuddled together in the middle. I stretched out my foot. My toe touched the small rip in the linen that I dared not poke in case I made it bigger. Gradually my eyes became used to the light. A small fire glowed in the hearth. We didn't often have fires. It was cheaper to warm ourselves downstairs and then race back to our room, bringing the warmth with us. I caught the thick, sweet smell of drying clothes.

There was a shadow sitting by the dresser, a Mama-shaped shadow. I'd always know that shape. Mama raised her arm and wiped her eyes. I heard her sniff and make a tiny sound like a sob. I wanted to shrug off the blanket, roll off the bed and go to comfort her, but my legs felt like they were still under the water, my eyes too. My eyelids drooped and when I woke up it was light.

My clothes were draped over the bedstead. I touched them. They were dry and smelt of wood smoke. I managed to sit up, though the inside of my head was still watery and when I breathed in, it felt like I was being poked with pins. I lay back down and stared at the brown water marks spreading down the walls from the eaves. I licked my dry lips. I tasted salt. Someone had fought the river for me. That someone was Mama.

I must have fallen asleep again because this time when I opened my eyes, Mama was sitting on the bed looking at me. She smiled.

"How are you?"

My stomach churned every time I moved and my

mouth tasted like I'd eaten a dead rat. I was alive, though. She stroked my cheek.

"Perhaps this will help?" She handed me my poppet. Its clothes were streaked with dirt and it had lost its hair and bonnet. "You dropped it in the boat before you went over."

I took it. "I told you it was lucky," I said.

Mama smiled. "Hopefully, more luck will be coming our way. Get dressed, Eve. We have to meet someone."

"Who?"

"Just get dressed, my darling."

My clothes were stiff from the river's mud even though Mama had tried to beat it out. She sprinkled a little of the scent she'd found in one of the rooms a few weeks ago over them. She made me wash my face in the bowl on the dresser, then washed her own.

"Where are we going?" I asked.

She turned to me. Water dripped off her hands and chin and for a moment I shivered, thinking of her throwing herself into the river after me.

"To see a man who would like to say sorry."

"Mama?"

"Get dressed, Eve."

The streets were busy and last night's rain had left the cobbles covered in slops. We headed towards Long

Southwark and away from the river. I was happy with that. Just hearing the splash of it against the bridge and the watermen's calls was making my stomach churn again. We stopped outside the Tabard Inn. He was waiting for us there. Who else could it have been? Of course, the man. *The* man. The man who had made me fall in.

He was older than Mama, much older. Maybe as old as Mistress Horstead's mother, who Mama said must be at least sixty. He was wearing dark leather breeches, woollen stockings and short leather boots that looked like they'd travelled more than even Mama. His shirt was white and stained, with a leather jerkin over the top. His grey curly hair was topped with a dark cap. The face underneath looked like someone had grabbed its skin and crumpled it together with an extra hard pinch for its nose. It was as red as sunset. The man's hands hung by his side and I noticed that half the little finger on his right hand was missing.

He nodded at Mama and she nodded back. He looked down at me.

"I'm glad you're recovered," he said.

He was glad? He should be glad! It was his fault that I'd nearly died in the first place! If he'd stayed in his seat my head wouldn't be throbbing and I wouldn't be tasting river. I dropped my eyes and stepped behind Mama. She has taught me good lessons about hiding my anger.

He gave me a little smile.

"I hope your mother told you that I want to make amends for yesterday. But first, let's eat."

Let's eat. At any other time, those words would have made me very happy. But this morning, my stomach seemed full of sludge. I didn't think I could ever eat again. We followed him across the courtyard into the inn. The landlord looked Mama up and down, then turned to the man.

"God save you, sir. How can I be of help to you and – your guests?" Another look at Mama and me.

"We need food. Didn't you say last night that you had bread and herrings?"

The landlord scurried away. Perhaps it was only me that noticed a woman who must have been his wife and a serving girl peering round the barrels at us. We sat down at a table, the man on one side, Mama and me on the other. A couple of moments later, the serving girl thumped three tankards of ale on the table. I took a sip of mine. It was weak and bitter.

The man said, "I didn't have an opportunity to introduce myself yesterday. My name is George Symons, currently of Southwark, previously of Portsmouth."

Of course, I knew where Southwark was. But Portsmouth? Perhaps it was one of the villages further down the Thames. He looked at me.

Mama nudged me. "Where are your manners, Eve?"

I wanted to say that they had floated away from me when George Symons had tried to kill me.

"You're too old to be shy, Eve," Mama said.

I wasn't shy. I was furious. Mama should know the difference.

"How old are you?" George Symons asked.

Mama nudged me harder. "Twelve," I said. Another nudge so hard I almost fell off the chair. "Sir," I added.

The serving girl thumped down a board with half a loaf of dark bread and a platter of fried herrings. George Symons picked one up and started to peel the flesh away from the bones. He piled it into a heap on the side of the platter. He turned the fish over and worked on the other side. The fish's head bobbed around, its eyes white and glazed. He pushed the platter towards us. Mama took a pinch of the fish and put it in her mouth.

"Eat," Mama said.

I shook my head.

George Symons carved a slice off the loaf and offered it to us. Mama tore the slice in two and gave the bigger piece to me. I nibbled the crust. The crumbs settled in my queasy stomach.

"Yesterday, in the river," George Symons said, "if it wasn't for your courage, you would be preparing for

27

your daughter's funeral today."

My throat closed up. I lay the bread down.

He leaned toward Mama. "It was like a miracle. You dived into the water like – like a porpoise. And I've seen porpoises." He laughed. The lines in his face smoothed out a little. "I have never seen a woman swim like that. Or indeed a man. Did you learn in your own land?"

Mama gave the tiniest of nods.

"A miracle." He stared out the window. "Even though I was born by the sea and raised by the sea, I cannot swim. Even though I knew my destiny was to sail on a ship, I still did not learn how to swim. Though why should I? It's better to drown quickly than splash around waiting for a ship that will never turn back for you."

He turned to look Mama in the eye. "I'd always known that there were dangers in the deep sea, far away from any known land. But once I … I was tipped into the water so close to shore, I swore I could see my mother and young sister crying out for me."

He banged his cup on the table. The serving girl brought another flagon of ale. "And butter," he called after her. "Have all the cows gone dry?"

The butter was slammed down next to the flagon and the girl walked away.

"Yesterday, in that boat, I was frightened," he said. "And I'm a grown man. I shouldn't admit that in front of women."

I'm a woman now?

"But I have nearly drowned before."

"How so?" Mama had taken the words from my mouth.

"Do you know the story of King Henry's *Mary Rose*?" he asked.

"No," Mama said. "Was she another of his wives?"

George Symons gave a smile so quick and bright I thought I'd imagined it. "She was a warship, Madam, one of his favourites. She fought many a battle for King Henry."

"And you were a sailor on her?" Mama asked.

"I'm a carpenter by trade. My father died when I was a child and I lived with my Uncle Francis. He was a carpenter, like my grandfather before him. My grandfather made a good living before King Henry moved his shipyard to Deptford, but there was still work enough for us in Portsmouth."

He filled his tankard and offered the flagon towards Mama, but we had barely sipped ours.

"The *Mary Rose* was built in Portsmouth. My grandfather helped fit her hull. If she hadn't sunk, she would have been an old woman now, nearly seventy. I saw her when she returned to Portsmouth after many years' service, heavier, stronger, ready for new wars."

I heard the clatter of horses outside in the yard. The

room would fill up soon with thirsty travellers and the man still hadn't got to the bit where he said sorry to me. He took another gulp of ale. Mama echoed him by taking a sip of her own drink. I followed, just letting the liquid touch my tongue.

"I was taken on as an apprentice carpenter on the *Mary Rose*. My uncle was the carpenter's assistant. I understand!" He lunged forward. I shot back. He leaned away and buried his face in his hands.

"I just want you to know that I understand how it feels when the water's got hold of you and is sucking you under. I understand what it's like to see every moment of your life before you, when you're sure that you will die."

Mama gave him a long look. She said, "How do you know this?"

"I was on board when the *Mary Rose* went down. The French were coming for us, more than two hundred ships sailing across the Solent towards us. We were one of eighty ships, waiting in Portsmouth harbour for them, proudly flying King Henry's banner. The king had spent his riches on us. His rose was even stamped into the cannon. And they were mighty cannon too. How could we ever be defeated?" He laughed. "The king himself had come down to see the spectacle. And it was a spectacle. The fields were filled with the royal pavilions and the brewhouses were working hard to keep the tankards full. The cannon were stoked and ready, the bill men were thumping their staffs on the earth, waiting for the chance to impale a Frenchman. I remember looking back and thinking that no man could break through our defences." He laughed again. I didn't know why. He didn't seem to find his tale funny.

"I should not have tested God," he said. "At first the wind was too slow and the sails were slack, but then it was like God sent us speed. We moved towards those French galleys."

As he spoke, the man's eyes were like the fish's, glazed to the outside world, as he fought the battle inside his head. Mama squeezed my hand under the table.

"My uncle's saw snapped and he sent me back to the carpenter's cabin for a fresh one. That saved my life, but not my uncle's. As I opened the cabin door, the boat tipped. I fell sideways and the water came."

"Was the boat hit?" Mama asked.

"No one knows why we went down. Some say a cannonball hit us, but I didn't feel the impact. Some say the men were unruly, but they were all good men. My uncle, he was good at his trade and proud to be serving the king. I do know that there were nets at the side of the ship. They were meant to stop the invaders boarding us, but the nets stopped our men getting out."

"How many men were lost?"

He threw back the rest of his ale. "Nearly five hundred boarded. Less than forty lived. The carpenter's cabin was on the main deck, so I had more time to reach the upper deck. I clung to the mizzenmast until a rowing boat came to rescue me. Those on the decks below had no chance."

I thought of Mama's grip round me, pulling me back up to life. I wanted to ask who helped him, but when I thought about being in the river yesterday, the water was pressing against my eyes again. I wondered if he felt the same when he told his story.

Mama said, "I'm sorry."

As he looked at Mama, his eyes came alive again. "I knew you would understand the pain."

He turned his gaze on me. "And you understand, don't you, Eve? That thin line between life and death?"

I realized I was nodding. I stopped myself. He had been the one who drew that line.

"I'm glad you agree." His sudden smile made me jolt. His teeth were the colour of underwater. "We do not know when our lives will be cut short, so we must make the most of this life before passing on to the next."

The travellers came into the room and pulled out chairs around the biggest table. The serving girl was summoned for ale and she still couldn't resist having a peep at me. I was tempted to make a face at her. My dead-dog face was especially ugly, but Mama had told me off last time she caught me doing it. She'd said that people look at us enough already.

George Symons had leaned in so close to Mama that his forehead almost touched hers.

"I need your help, madam."

"My help?"

"To make our fortune."

One of the travellers laughed loudly and scraped back his chair. Mama turned to look at him then back at George Symons.

"My fortune?"

"Your feat yesterday was astounding, madam. Please believe me. It's your pathway to riches."

Mama's face didn't change, but she tore bread from her slice and used it to scoop up some fish. She washed it down with a good sip of ale.

"There's treasure to be found," he said.

This time I really did make my dead-dog face. You cannot live in Southwark without hearing every lost-treasure tale there is.

Mama said, "Would you have me dive back into the

Thames to find gold? It's rich in horse carcasses, but I would not call that treasure."

George Symons laughed so loudly that some of the travellers looked round at him. Mama's joke wasn't that funny.

"No," he said. "I'm not talking about the Thames. You would need to leave Southwark."

Mama grasped my hand again. "This is my home," she said. "I will not leave it."

"Home, madam? A home is where there is more than this" – he held his forefinger and thumb close together as if he was going to pinch Mama – "between having a warm bed and sleeping on the street. Home is where you have food in your pantry and a fire in your hearth. That is the home that riches will bring you."

Last year, some minstrels set up a puppet show next to the baiting ring by the river. Every time I decided to leave, the story would catch me again and I knew that I'd have to stay until the end. I'm not sure if Mama fully believed him, but her face said that she couldn't stop listening.

"You can travel with your daughter, of course," George Symons said.

"Travel where?" Mama asked.

"Southampton."

"Where's Southampton?" I hadn't meant the words

to come out. Mama was always reminding me that I should never interrupt adults when they were talking together. Mama and George Symons looked at me then at each other.

"It's where you will meet the guide to our treasure," George Symons said.

"You want me to go to an unknown place and seek out a guide to help me find hidden treasure. That's not a plan. That's a children's tale." Mama stood up. "Come on, Eve. Mistress Horstead will be missing us."

"Madam, please." George Symons stood too and placed a hand on Mama's shoulder. Her eyes narrowed and he quickly removed it. "Just hear me out."

He sat down. I watched to see what Mama would do. The travellers were quiet, watching us too. She lowered herself, slowly, to make sure that he knew she was doing him a favour.

He continued, "When the *Mary Rose* sank, she took some of the king's best cannon. There were chests of pewter plate and, some said, gold. Some Venetians were paid to lift her soon after she'd sunk, but the mast snapped and she tipped back into the water. It didn't stop the men drinking Portsmouth dry. Two years later, another Venetian came – Peter Corsi. He brought with him three black men from Guinea in Africa."

Mama frowned. "Three black men?"

"Black." He tapped Mama's hand. "As coal."

I had once seen Mama slap a drunk man for doing the same. Mama removed her hand from the table. "What did he bring these black men to do?"

George Symons smiled again. This smile was slower so I was ready for it. "To dive, of course."

A BOAT AND A CART

George Symons had a plan. I wonder now if his plan was even bigger than I had realized. Perhaps he had seen Mama in London long before we shared a boat with him on the Thames. Perhaps he had been following her, hoping for a chance to talk to her and had paid our fare so we would travel with him. Perhaps he'd made the boat wobble on purpose, so he could test her skill. But then I remembered his voice and the look on his face as the boat rolled in the current and I knew that part wasn't faked.

That morning in the Tabard, he told us the story of Jacques Francis. He'd been the best of the three black divers, going deeper than any other.

Mama interrupted him. "Are you telling me this because you want me to dive into the harbour for cannon?"

"The *Mary Rose* sank in Portsmouth," George Symons said. "But there was another boat that sank close to Southampton a year later. She was called the *Sancta Maria and Sanctus Edwardus*. She belonged to a Venetian merchant and was carrying a rich cargo. Peter Corsi organized the salvage for this ship too. Jacques Francis dived there again. It didn't end well."

I saw the flicker of disappointment cross Mama's face before her expression went blank. "He died."

"No." George Symons smiled, the sort of smile that people often hid behind their hands. "He lived, but the merchants who lost their cargo claimed that Corsi had not given them everything the divers had taken from the ship. I believe that not only did Corsi keep hold of some of the cargo for himself, but that there are still riches waiting to be taken from that boat."

"Why would you believe that?" asked Mama.

"They were rich merchants, Mistress Cartwright, but they would not have spent all that money on divers if all they had lost was leather and tin. There's gold down there, Mistress Cartwright. Gold."

Mama's face said nothing. "So why didn't they get it back?"

"There was a court case. The merchants accused Corsi of stealing their cargo. Corsi made Jacques Francis swear before the court that Corsi was an honest man and would do no such thing. The rich merchants didn't like this. They denounced Jacques as a slave and an infidel and said his testimony wasn't to be trusted."

Mama muttered under her breath. It was something about knowing those words well herself.

"Jacques knows where that ship lies," George Symons continued. "He knows how deep the water is and what treasure waits for us in the wreckage. If we can win his trust, he will be our guide."

"I feel that we should leave him be," Mama said.

"Perhaps we should," George Symons agreed. "Perhaps we should leave the gold to sink into the river bed and never be claimed. Or perhaps, *you* could be rich?"

A look flickered across Mama's face. She was always saying to me, *Trust no one*. As George Symons shoved a wad of bread in his mouth, I wondered how much she was starting to trust him.

"What is expected of me?" she asked.

What *was* expected of Mama? Well, George Symons explained that there was a man who assisted an elderly apothecary in a shop near Christ's Hospital in London, and he was sure that this man was Jacques Francis. George Symons had tried to talk with him, but the man had insisted that he had never been a diver. He claimed his name was Anthony and he'd been a gentleman's servant in Winchester. George Symons had recognized him, though. After the *Mary Rose* had sunk, he'd spent hours sitting on the wall of Portsmouth harbour watching the men dive and surface. It may have been more than twenty years ago, but George Symons said that he could not forget that face.

The apothecary was called Nicholas Balcombe. When George Symons had made enquiries, he'd found out that Master Balcombe had a second shop in Southampton that had been closed for a while. He'd instructed Jacques Francis to bring the remaining medicines and equipment to London and then wait for a shipment in Southampton before returning to London.

We were to head to Southampton in February when "Anthony" would be there. George Symons would organize lodgings for us with his cousin, a widow with a sick daughter who would welcome our help and company. We were to continue with our usual lives in London until he came to tell us that all the arrangements were complete.

Five months passed. I had almost forgotten about the plan. Then Mama shook me awake in the middle of the night, or at least, it seemed like it was in the middle of the night to me. I was happy to be roused. I had been dreaming that I was back on the river, in the boat, rolling from side to side. I sat up so quickly I almost bounced my head against my mother's.

"George Symons is waiting," she said.

"How do you know?"

"He came to find me last night to tell me all was ready."

"It's still night."

I could feel her smile in the darkness. "No, *mpendwa*, it's close to morning. Get dressed."

Mama had already packed our scant possessions – the chemise she'd bought at the rag fair, a comb, a small blanket and, of course, my lucky poppet. We sat side by side on the saggy bed, pinning up our curls and tucking them beneath our bonnets.

"Now we're respectable," she said.

As Mama straightened the bed, I could hear her small purse of coins clinking. I looked out of the window. It was that moment at dawn when the stars are bright, but there's a faded edge around the darkness. The moon looked like someone had clipped a chip off its side, but it was bright enough to see the shadow of George Symons waiting below. I hoped Mistress Sleet wouldn't choose that moment to open her window and empty her chamber pot.

Mama and I crept downstairs. We went carefully because the steps are noisy. Also, Mama said that sometimes guests had so much ale they couldn't make it up to their rooms, and the last thing we wanted to do was to kick a sleeping merchant who would shriek so hard that he brought Master Horstead running. Thankfully our passage that morning was clear.

Downstairs, Mama told me to stay by the door. I would rather have crouched over the embers of the fire to take as much warmth from them as I could. Even I knew that February was no time to travel. But the best time to dive is May and George Symons had said that we had to be sure we had enough time to make Jacques Francis trust us. That gave us three months. Three months until we'd have riches beyond our imagination, he'd said. Beyond my imagination? As I did my best to imagine them, Mama returned with the kitchen boy stumbling behind her. She opened her purse and gave him a coin. When she closed the door, I heard him bolt it behind us again.

This was it. This was the end of our time at the Boar's Head. I'd lived in enough places to never feel sad when I was leaving them. It was the same this time, except I couldn't help thinking – when we returned to Southwark, would we be rich enough to buy our own tavern?

I whispered to Mama, "Everything will be fine, won't it?"

She bobbed down and kissed my head. "It's a new adventure, Eve."

Yes, I was an adventurer.

George Symons greeted us with a grunt and hurried ahead. As we scurried after him, through the dark streets of Southwark, I repeated it to myself. *I am an adventurer! I am an adventurer. When I return, I will be rich!*

Then I realized that we were heading towards the river. Wasn't that the wrong way? We were supposed to be heading south, not across to London.

"I am an adventurer! I am adventurer!" I said the words out loud as the smell of the river grew stronger, but the words weren't loud enough to hide my thumping heart.

George Symons was moving quickly through the grey morning shadows. Mama hurried to catch up with him. We passed a baker's shop. The oven must have been lit already because I could smell warm bread. The mastiffs were baying by the bear garden, where people watched dogs fight captive bears for fun. And I could hear the river whispering to me, the waves lapping at the jetty and the creak of ropes as boats tried to free themselves and float away.

The stars were fading into the morning sky as we came on to Bankside. I found Mama's hand and squeezed it.

"Are we going on a boat?" I asked.

She nodded. "But don't worry, *mpendwa*. It's a big

one. It belongs to a rich merchant who's sailing back home via Southampton. Master Symons says that it's our quickest route."

My stomach started bumping around just thinking about it. It wasn't just wherries that threw you into the sea. We were here because George Symons had told us about a big warship tipping over.

"Wait here." He walked towards the wharf.

We were at the steps near Paris Gardens. I could see the bigger boats anchored across the river, while the wherries and rowing boats bumped against each other and the wharf. The sailors were already busy, calling to each other in languages I didn't understand. *Laranjas*. Was that oranges? Maybe Mama would know.

"Mama?"

"Shush!" She seemed to be stretching towards the river, listening with her whole body.

"We're ready." George Symons was back. He was with a short man whose head barely reached the carpenter's shoulder. In the dawn gloom, it was easier to smell him than to see him. I wished Mama hadn't sold all her little lavender bags, though it would take a whole cartload of lavender to make the short man smell good. He was staring at Mama. As usual, she stared back. The way he looked at her made me want to turn back to the Boar's Head. She put an arm around my shoulders and I felt the solid strength of her body. I had to be more like Mama and remember that adventurers didn't give up simply because they didn't like the look (or smell) of people.

The sailor said something to Mama. It was in a different language and the words didn't sound like anything I knew. Mama didn't reply. Why should she? She only spoke English to strangers. He laughed loudly and I was hit by the smell of his breath. He came up closer to Mama and said something else.

Mama grabbed my hand, spun round and marched away. What? Adventurers didn't…

George Symons raced after us. If I ever repeated the words he shouted, Mama would have taken me to the edge of the city and left me there. Mama just carried on walking. George Symons grabbed her arm and we jolted to a stop. Mama didn't like anyone to touch her and I saw her warning-face flash on. George Symons wisely let her go.

She said, "I'm not travelling with Portuguese."

"Not all the crew are Portuguese."

"The Portuguese stole me from my family. I will not travel with them. I do not believe that they will take me where I want to go."

George Symons dared to touch Mama's arm again, but gently. "Please take the boat. You will be safe. You're only travelling to Southampton."

"I would not travel across to London with them."

"You have my word."

"I don't trust your word. I don't trust anybody's word."

She started walking again, pulling me after her.

"Then our whole plan is ruined," he said.

"Yes," Mama said. "Our whole plan is ruined if there is only one way to travel to Southampton."

"He already has my money! I had to pay him extra too, because you're a woman."

Mama laughed. "Yes, a woman on a boat is supposed to bring bad luck, unless you've stolen her away from her family."

A little smile played on George Symons' lips. "But you've already given up your lodgings. Will you and your child walk the streets?"

Mama stared him down. "It wouldn't be the first time."

That was true, but I had hoped that fighting the giant rat in the grain store would be the last time. We once stole into a sheepcote and I'd spent the night cuddling up to a ewe for warmth. That hadn't been so bad, even if the owner was most displeased to see us in the morning.

Mama walked quickly like she already knew our destination. George Symons puffed by the side of us.

"Please," he said. "Stop."

Mama stopped. The bridge was up ahead. The tide was low and the water between the piers seemed almost still. Grey smoke curled from the merchants' houses above the arches. The gates into London must have been open because there was already a queue of carts waiting to cross over.

Mama turned to face him, hands on her hips. "I have stopped, Master Symons. What do you wish to say to me?"

"There's a dyer's son," he said. "I met him in the Saracen last week. He'd come up from Winchester to deliver alum to Cloth Fair. He was waiting for some dresses to be made up for his sisters and mother. If he hasn't already left, perhaps I can persuade him to deliver you to Winchester. From there, it's an easy journey on to Southampton. Does that route suit you better?"

"Yes," Mama said. "It does."

"He's lodging at the Old Swan. Shall we take our chances on the bridge?"

I nodded so hard, I'm surprised my head didn't bounce off and hit a wherryman.

I only had to take one step on to the bridge to know that I wasn't in Southwark any more. Southwark looks like a giant has wrapped his arms around it and squeezed. The houses lean towards each other, squashed in the middle and bulging out at the top so you can almost reach out from the top storeys and touch each other's hands over the road. The alleys wind and wriggle between the houses, sometimes barely wide enough for a starving dog, sometimes leading to a sudden dead end. These are the haunts of vagabonds and thieves and those with no bed, or even a sheepcote, for the night.

The houses and shops on the bridge are different. It's like the giant clapped the buildings into a block and poked a stick through the length of it to make a pathway. The top storeys of the houses swell over the road, and over the water as well.

The gateway loomed above me. A few years ago, we were lodging in an attic off Long Southwark. Our tiny window faced out towards the river and the first thing I'd see as the sun came up was the dark circles of the traitors' heads on their long stems sprouting out from the roof of the gate. I had never longed to get any closer, but here I was, staring up at the bulging shapes. I used to think that traitors turned that black colour when they died, but Mama said the heads were preserved in tar to make them last longer. Birds swooped around them, looking for, well, untarred bits and left their own white decorations. Today there were five heads. When we lived in Tooley Street, I once counted more than twenty.

I looked away towards the rainbow house in the middle of the bridge. That's not its proper name, but it should have been. It covers the whole width of the bridge with an arch in the middle to pass through. Two carts were jammed in front of the arch. They had been trying to edge past each other, but their wheels had become locked together. The carters were yelling and so were all the people trying to get past them. George Symons went to push his way through the crowds, but Mama didn't follow. I was happy to wait, staring at the colourful house and its strange onion-topped towers and gold weather vanes. If I was a good adventurer, would I have enough money to buy a house like that? If I did, it wouldn't be over a river.

The carters finally decided to take action. The one heading south persuaded his horse to back up to let the other one pass. After they'd exchanged a few more curses, the way was clear. Well, clear apart from all the other carts and people on horseback and beggars and customers weaving their way in and out of the shops.

"Hurry up!" George Symons threw the words back at us. "He may have already left."

VISITORS IN THE NIGHT

The dyer's son was called Valentine. He looked like one of the fat-faced apprentices who roamed through Southwark after twilight. Pockmarks were scattered across his cheeks as if an enemy had thrown a fistful of small pebbles at his face. He licked his lips as if they were covered in London's best salt. When he saw us, I thought a nail had come loose in his jaw because his mouth fell open and stayed that way. When he talked, his breath came in whistles and with too much spit. I was glad it was George Symons sitting opposite him, not me.

Valentine was the person who would carry us down to Southampton. I started to think that we'd be better travelling by boat. The deal was easier than expected. The dresses were ready for collection, but Valentine owed money – he'd been to Bartholomew Fair and had been caught out by the card sharps. He would be happy to take us if George Symons paid the seamstress and his bill at the Old Swan. George Symons wasn't happy, but the day was passing and we had only reached London. He didn't have time to argue. So we went to Cloth Fair to collect the dresses and then back to the Old Swan to pay his bill. Valentine also needed money for lodgings on the way – enough for two rooms because it wouldn't be decent for him to share a room with Mama and me – for three nights, just to be safe.

"How come George Symons is paying for everything?" I asked Mama.

"Because he expects us to make his fortune."

The sun was high and Valentine insisted that we ate before we left and also got extra food to take with us – again George Symons paid. The landlord served us bowls of pottage and boiled eels, and wrapped three meat pies for us to take away. Valentine reached out his hand for them, but Mama got there first. Valentine narrowed his eyes but said nothing.

Valentine's horse was called Succour. He was pale brown with thick legs and a long, knotty mane. It took a while to fit the harness. Succour had been enjoying his freedom in London as much as his owner had and didn't take kindly to being reminded that he was a carthorse. I wasn't sure if it was because he didn't like the harness or he didn't like Valentine. The cart was a box on a platform balanced on a shaft between two big wheels with a canopy to pull over if it rained. As it bumped and lurched around the courtyard, I knew that Mama and I would be thrown around like sacks of wheat.

Still, the adventurer inside me gave a little excited shiver. We would soon be on our way. Well, as soon as we'd finished waiting for the farmer to herd his cows across the bridge. They were thin creatures with sad faces as if they knew they were heading to market. George Symons walked to the end of Long Southwark with us. He pressed a purse of money into Mama's hands. I saw Valentine's eyes flick towards it and away again.

George Symons bent towards Mama. "You know what's expected of you?"

Mama nodded.

"Good. I'll be with you soon after May Day."

He bent down and cupped his hand to help Mama scramble into the cart, then lifted me up and plonked me next to her. He went up to Valentine and I saw his thick, rough finger jab Valentine's shoulder.

"Do not forget your deal!"

Valentine nodded, then pulled at Succour's reins. George Symons strode back towards Bankside. We were finally off.

Mama and I took turns sitting on the package of dresses, but it didn't do much to cushion the bumps.

The going was slow, not much faster than we could have walked, even though Succour was pulling at his reins like he wanted to gallop away. I'm glad he didn't. Southwark was still in sight and my bottom was already bruised.

Soon we were passing through fields, bare branches and tufts of grass. The mud on the highway was frozen into ridges and the cartwheels jolted over every one. Mama sat me on her lap in the hope it might weigh us down. Instead, it just hurt her more as she landed harder every time we bumped. In the front, Valentine was whistling away to himself. He had a thick leather cushion underneath *his* bottom.

We stopped once before nightfall because I needed to go to the toilet. Mama was cross. She thought Valentine wouldn't wait for us. Just in case, she took the pies with her. Later, when I tried to eat one, the jolting meant my mouth was never where I expected it to be and I kept poking myself in the cheek. It didn't matter. I wasn't hungry anyway. I was starting to feel sick and I was too hot, even though Valentine was now wearing a cape over his coat. Mama touched my forehead and glanced towards Valentine. There'd been plague in London six years before I was born. Folk continued to be suspicious.

Twilight was turning the world into shadows again. The air seemed to freeze across my hot face. Mama wrapped me tight in my cloak and stroked my back as I lay across her lap.

"There's an inn ahead," Valentine called back to us. I'd thought he'd forgotten we were there. "I stayed there on my way up to London." He steered Succour into the yard. "I'll go in and enquire about rooms."

He climbed down from the seat, stretched and tied Succour to a post.

"Pass me the money so I can secure our rooms."

"I thought we paid the bill afterwards," Mama said.

"We want two rooms," Valentine said. "Good rooms too, as Master Symons instructed. I need to show the innkeeper that we can pay."

The purse clanked in Mama's hands. "How much do you need?"

"I don't know. Pass me the purse and I'll return it."

My mouth wouldn't open. My lips wouldn't move or I would have shouted *no!* Mama saw me trying to speak and felt my forehead again.

She handed Valentine the money. "Go. And come back quickly."

He strode off towards the inn. I felt like I'd been lying too close to the fire while an angry cook pummelled me with a cudgel. I wasn't sure I could get out of the cart even if he found us a room fit for the Queen.

Mama lay next to me and covered us both with her cloak.

"Be patient," she said. "You'll be in a soft bed soon."

An owl called and further away I could hear the tinkle of water. There must have been stables too, as Succour was answering faint whinnies with a jerk of the cart. I fell asleep and woke up to voices. One was Mama's, the other was a man's. The tips of my fingers were stinging with cold and every time my body moved, I thought lightning had struck my head.

"The horse is to be stabled," the man said. He must be the ostler.

"And what about us?"

"He didn't tell me he had passengers."

"Then please go and find him, sir. He has instructions to find us lodgings."

"He's long gone to his bed. He enjoyed the landlord's kegs very well indeed."

I must have groaned because they stopped talking and a pool of light fell over me.

"Is she sick?" the ostler asked.

"Just a chill." There was a quiver in Mama's voice. "She fell into the river a few months ago and it weakened her chest."

I saw the ostler shake his head. "We cannot bring London sickness into the house."

"It's just a chill," said my mother.

"It always starts with just a chill," he replied.

"She does not have the plague! It's just a chill!"

"You cannot come into the house."

"Then what are we to do?"

The ostler untied Succour from the post and led her – and me – over to the stables. He opened a wide door and we went in. I could hear Mama following behind.

"We are not vagrants!" Her voice sounded harsh and loud. "We cannot sleep in a bush! We have money!"

"Where is your money?" the ostler asked.

"It's with that rogue!" Mama said.

The ostler started to unbuckle Succour from the harness. "Then your argument is with him."

Mama's voice was very quiet. "I don't want an argument. I just want a warm place to stay for the night."

I closed my eyes, though it was more like my eyes were sinking into my head and the skin was closing up over them like a scab.

We slept in the stable's hayloft. The ostler brought us blankets, bread and a little soup. I know now that it was his wife's doing. She'd come into the stables to find him, seen us and berated him for refusing us help. She even brewed up medicine and made a poultice for me, though Mama said she wouldn't come close enough to touch me, even though Mama showed her my neck to prove I was free from plague boils.

I should remember more of those hours, but my memories are like the smoke from the merchants' houses on the bridge. They curl up out of my head and disappear. I remember smells – hay, dung, horse sweat. There was my sweat too, because my clothes were wet, like I'd just been pulled out of the river again. If Mama had tried to take those clothes off me, my skin would have peeled away with them. Mama sang, I remember that. Her face was close to mine, her hand stroking my hair. I remember a cockerel crowing and another one answering its call before I closed my eyes.

I woke up in full light. I lay there in my damp hay-covered shroud and tried to work out what was missing. Of course – it was Mama. My body was still tender and heavy, but I managed to drag it over to the hatch to look down into the stable. She wasn't there. Nor was Succour. They must be attaching him to the cart again. I knew from yesterday that Succour would be putting up a fight. Mama must be with Valentine, telling him exactly what she thought of him making us sleep in a stable.

Unless they'd left me. No, Mama would never do that, not even if I really did have the plague. I touched my neck. I couldn't feel any lumps, but maybe there were other signs I didn't know about. Maybe Mama was persuading the ostler's wife to brew me up more medicine?

Hooves clattered in the yard outside. Someone shrieked. Was that Mama? My heart beat harder. I wriggled over to the ladder that led down into the stable and grasped the top rung, but the inside of my head was curling smoke again. My eyes were blurry and the sweats had returned. I lay on my back. I could hear shouting now and the voice was Mama's. The hooves grew quieter and quieter until they were gone.

"Eve?" Mama's head poked out from the hatch.

I turned my head and opened my eyes. "Are we leaving now?"

She climbed up and dropped on to the hay next to me.

"He's gone, Eve. He's left us. The ostler's wife came to warn me, but he would have run me down rather than stop for us. He has all our money." She lay down. "He has everything."

I knew then that she was sinking. When I fell out of the wherry, it felt like I was being pulled to the bottom of the river. When Mama sank, it was like everything was being pulled back inside her. She couldn't talk or eat, and I don't think she always knew who I was.

Sometimes it lasted for a day or two. Once, it was for nearly a month. *Please don't sink. Please don't sink.* When she was falling, I knew I couldn't catch her. We lay side by side and I listened to the comings and goings in the stable below while the sky changed from pale grey to dark.

At twilight, the ostler's wife brought us soup and a little bread. My head was hurting and my legs were heavy, but I knew I was getting well again. Mama though, had barely moved. Was this how our big adventure ended? Abandoned and penniless in a stable? No! I was an adventurer! Adventures had to be difficult and dangerous. I couldn't call myself an adventurer if everything went well. So, what was I going to do? First, I needed to make sure we had food and board until we could travel. Second, I had to work out how we would travel. Would we continue to look for treasure in Southampton or return to Southwark and the grain store?

The next morning, the ostler's wife brought us some apples. I offered to help her in her garden as payment for the food and board, but she said that there was little to do in February. But she was happy for me to help with the sewing and brought me a big basket of sheets and aprons to mend. I asked Mama if she would sew with me, but she tucked her knees under her chin and closed her eyes. I worked for as long as there was light, peeping down from the hatch to check who was bringing in horses to stable. When it became too dark to sew, I tried to feed Mama a little bread, but she refused.

"Please, Mama," I whispered. "Just enough to keep you strong."

The stable door opened. I peered down. A man was leading a horse with one hand and holding a lantern with the other. He wore a heavy riding cloak over a dark doublet and hose and a high soft-crowned cap. He was humming to himself as he unsaddled his horse and filled a trough with feed. As he lifted his head, his cap dropped into the trough. I squeezed back a giggle. He held up the lantern, but missed me in the shadows. I saw then that the man's skin was as dark as Mama's. The man was black, like Mama and me. I had seen people like us in Southwark; musicians playing at the fairs or servants following behind rich people's carriages. But this man wasn't wearing servants' clothes and I couldn't imagine him playing the trumpet for tokens. He finished settling his horse then made his way to the inn.

"Mama?"

Her eyes were open, but she was as still as if she was sleeping.

"I've just seen a man like us! His horse is below. Should I talk to him?"

She said nothing.

"Mama?" I squeezed a handful of hay and felt a sharp end pierce my palm. I let it go. "Do you think he may be the man we're looking for? Do you think God brought luck to us?"

Mama turned on her side and rolled away from me. I had to be patient. Mama always surfaced again in the end.

"Mama?"

"Deixe-me dormir."

She wanted me to let her sleep. Her eyes closed and she curled tighter. I wasn't ready to sleep, though. I climbed down into the stable. My knees were wobbly and I clung to the ladder so hard that chips of wood splintered into my skin. I eased open the stable door and ran across the dark yard.

"Sir!" I called. "Sir!"

The man slowed but did not stop. I pushed my aching body to make one last burst of speed and almost threw myself in front of his feet. He looked for a moment like he was going to step right over me. He bent down and helped me up. His eyes widened when he saw me and he let me go so quickly I almost fell over again.

"I've no money," he said. "Do not bother trying to beg it from me."

How many people did he see that looked like us, but he still thought badly of me. Tiredness and anger took over.

"I'm not a beggar!"

"So what do you want?"

"I…" Was this the moment to ask him about a wrecked ship and its treasure? What if it wasn't Jacques Francis? "My Mama and I are staying in the stable," I said. "And I saw you and…"

"So you're a spy, then. Or a thief, watching to see where I leave my valuables."

"No, I am not a spy! Or a thief! I just thought … I thought I might know you."

He bent down, his face close to mine. His skin was coated with the grey dust of travel. His eyes were tinged with red. A small pearl earring was like a spot of light on his right ear.

"You don't know me," he said.

He walked towards the inn, pushed open the door and went inside. I crept over to the window and watched as he sat down at a table close to the kitchen. Was it really Jacques Francis? If George Symons was right, the diver would definitely have to travel this way.

"Why are you out here?"

I jumped so hard I almost separated from my skin. It was a girl. She had a round face that looked pale under the moonlight. Her smile touched her eyes and she cocked her head sideways. I realized that she was waiting for an answer. Behind her, the ostler had taken charge of a couple of horses and was leading them to the stables.

"Because she's outstayed her welcome," he muttered.

The girl giggled. The hem from her hood was falling crooked over her face. She pushed down her muffler to talk to me. I stared at her. I'd seen that face before! I was sure!

"If you give me a penny," she said, "I can ask my brother, Griffin, to read your charts."

That's when I knew who she was. It was the drummer girl!

"Why are you staring at me?" she asked.

"I saw you before. At Bartholomew Fair."

"Did Griffin read your charts then?"

"No."

"That's why you've had bad luck."

"How do you know I've had bad luck?"

"Because you're sleeping in the stable."

"Gina!" A man's voice came from the door to the inn. "Where are you?"

"That's my brother. He's like a dragon when he's hungry." She turned her head, shouting, "Just coming!"

"Your name's Gina," I said.

"No. It's Elizabeth, like Elizabeth Regina. But everybody's Elizabeth, so I'm Gina. What's your name?"

"Eve."

Gina looked me up and down, thoughtfully. "Do you have a skill, Eve?"

"A skill?"

"Can you juggle, sing, walk the tightrope?"

"No."

"Ah," she said. "That's a pity. I thought perhaps we could be of help to each other."

"Gina!" Griffin really did sound like he was ready to breathe fire.

"Sorry I can't help you." Gina moved away.

"Mama has a skill," I said quickly. "She can dive into the deepest water and survive."

"Is your mother a fish?" Gina clapped her hands. "Because if she is, that would make you a mermaid." She looked down at my legs. "We could always make you a fish tail. We could charge half a penny to see you and—"

I laughed. "I'm not a mermaid. I fell into the River Thames and almost drowned. Mama dived in to save me."

"You fell into the Thames? And you lived?"

"Yes, right by the bridge. At high tide."

Her eyes widened. She pinched my cart-bruised arm and I shrieked.

"No, you're definitely not a ghost," she said. "Not many people come out alive from there. That is a skill indeed. Where are you headed?"

"Towards Southampton. Well, we were before the wicked dyer's son rode off with all our money." My mouth carried on moving even though my brain wanted to hold it back. "We've been told there's treasure in the waters nearby. Mama's going to dive in and find it."

"Your mama's diving for treasure in Southampton." Gina said it like it was an everyday matter. "How does your mama know where to look?"

I opened my mouth again and glanced towards the window. The man had gone.

"It's probably just a sailors' tale," I said.

"But you're still going down there?"

"We have to keep moving around all the time. We thought it would make things better for us. We would do anything to have our own home."

"If the wicked dyer's son left you, how will you get there now?"

"Gina!" Griffin really did roar.

She gave me a wide smile. "If I don't go, Griffin will come looking for me. You really don't want to meet him, the mood he's in."

She ran off towards the inn. I stayed by the window,

watching as Gina and Griffin settled themselves at a table. Griffin had a thin face and reminded me of the cows we'd seen being driven over the bridge. Though something about him made me think that he wouldn't be the one who ended up at market. They turned to look at me, then leaned in close to talk.

I made my way back to the hayloft. The horse looked up from the trough as if it was wondering why I was disturbing its peace. I climbed up and sat next to Mama. She was curled up tight, sleeping. The moon had shifted so it cut across half her face. I stroked flecks of straw out of her hair.

"We are adventurers, Mama. We are adventurers."

THE BAG OF BEADS

"We'll take you to Southampton." Gina's head poked through the hatch to the hayloft. "We have to leave soon, though."

The head disappeared and it was replaced by a tray held high.

"Take it! Before I drop it all!"

Gina had brought two pies, still warm by the smell of them, and a flagon of... I flicked up the lid. "Is that milk?"

"Fresh from the cow," she replied.

I took the tray and Gina followed it into the loft.

Mama was sitting up, but she was nowhere near the surface yet. She'd only just pushed off from the bottom. Gina went and crouched next to her.

"Is she sick?"

I nodded.

"I'll fetch Griffin."

"No, please—" But she was gone and back a few

moments later with her brother. He nodded to me. A good meal and a warm bed for the night hadn't made him any happier.

"Your mother is melancholic. Her humours are off balance," he said. "She needs warmth and water to redress her balance and, perhaps, an infusion of hellebore. We have some with us."

"Are you an apothecary?" I asked.

Gina laughed. "We can fix your humours and grind your knifes. We can even throw six apples in the air and catch them one by one with our eyes closed."

There was another little laugh. It had come from Mama, though her head was still bowed.

Gina broke off a chunk of pie and put it in Mama's hand and raised Mama's hand to her mouth. I saw Mama take a little bite.

"See, she's getting better already," Gina said. "Are we ready to leave, Griffin?"

"Yes. Straight away."

It was hard to manoeuvre Mama down from the hayloft. Her legs flopped around and she almost kicked Griffin in the head. I heard him swear under his breath. Finally, we were outside. They were travelling by horse and cart too. Their cart was packed with chests and packages.

"Some of it's ours," Gina said. "But we also carry things between towns for other people."

We settled Mama in the back and covered her in blankets. Her head rested on a soft bag that I was sure must have been full of lavender. Griffin rode Anastasia, an old mottled horse. I gripped the seat next to Gina.

We spent one more night on the road as we didn't want to arrive at Southampton after curfew. Also, Anastasia wasn't impressed with her heavier load and was walking like her hooves were made of glass. We lodged with one of Gina and Griffin's cousins in Basing, a mile off the highway. The road was so bumpy, I thought the cart was going to tip right over.

Gina's cousin gave Mama and me a curious look until Gina told them about our mission and then she couldn't be more friendly. Griffin and the cousin's husband went out into the dark and came back shortly after with three rabbits. I watched as Griffin took a sharp knife, skinned them and prepared them for the pot. He turned to see me watching and brought the cleaver down so hard it made me blink.

Mama and I slept in the loft room above the buttery. It was cold, but they left us with a pile of blankets. As I cuddled into Mama, she put her arms around me and sighed. Next morning, Gina brewed Mama an infusion of herbs scooped from one of the sacks in the back of the cart. She refused to leave Mama until every drop was swallowed. I was also plied with medicine to make sure the last of my fever had broken.

Next stop, Southampton.

Travellers arriving from the south into London are met with tarred traitors' heads on poles on the bridge gatehouse. There's no such welcome to Southampton. We crunched along the gravel highway and waited our turn to pass over a bridge and through a great stone gateway. It was decorated with a painting of Queen Elizabeth and two more of people I didn't recognize. One of them looked like a giant. George Symons hadn't mentioned that there were giants in Southampton. I hoped they were friendly. On top of the gateway, instead of heads, there were fat white gulls, squawking and jostling for space on the ledges. Just like in London, walls stretched out from the gates to surround the town. Griffin paid the toll and we passed through.

I took a deep breath in. In London the air is still, caught in the twists between the alleyways and below the overhanging gables. Here, it felt like there was space for the breeze to dance. A road stretched down from the stone gate that looked like the town's main highway, lined with shops and taverns. There was a church spire down to the left and another on the right. That was the way we turned, on to a square. The church was on one side of the square and houses clustered round the other three sides. In the middle was a building on wooden pillars and below that, the ground was stained with blood from the fish market. The market had finished for the day, but I could still smell it. Dogs were skittering around the cobbles, bursting through the gulls searching for scraps. High on the hill, was a castle. I imagined standing on the keep and being able to look out across the water. I wondered if they could see the shipwreck from there.

"Where are you lodging?" Gina asked.

I looked at Mama. It often takes a while for her to find her thoughts when she is surfacing.

"Our lodgings in Southampton, Mama. Where are they?"

Mama frowned, then smiled. "He said we should go to Widow Primmer on East Street."

Griffin nodded. "I know the house."

Mama stayed in the cart while Griffin led Anastasia. Gina and I fell in behind. I knew that I would be sorry to leave her.

"Try and make sure your mother stays warm," Gina said. "Griffin says that the melancholic personality is prone to the cold. And take her for walks by the river too."

"Thank you," I said. "I'm not sure how Mama and I would have survived if we hadn't met you."

Suddenly, I had a thought. I dipped into my pocket and pulled out my poppet. It was battered and dirty and didn't look much of a gift. I offered her to Gina.

"We bought her at Bartholomew Fair. I know she doesn't look much, but the woman said it would bring us luck. And it has. It brought us you. I thought you might like some luck too."

Gina shook her head. "I can't take it."

"Please do." I dropped the poppet in her apron pocket. "Shall we catch up with your brother and Mama?"

Gina touched my arm. "I … I have something to show you. It's not a present, but Griffin told me that you must see it."

She opened her hand. She must have been holding it all this time. It was a small bag, made of smooth, wool-spun worsted, with no decoration. Gina loosened the drawstring and let me look inside.

"Beads?" I asked. They were wooden ones, enough to make a decent necklace. "What are they for?"

Gina took a breath. "Griffin said that they're to remind you of your debt."

"My debt?"

She swallowed so loudly, I almost thought it was

my own throat. "Griffin says that we have fed you, transported you, found overnight lodgings for you and treated your maladies. This has been at cost to ourselves and we're not rich people."

She picked a bead out and held it close to her eyes. "Each bead is worth a penny. He's going to add a bead a day because he says that's another day he – we – don't have the money he spent on you and your mama. He says the last day for payment is May Day."

She dropped the bead back into the bag and drew the string tight so the beads bulged against the thick fabric. When the strings were loose again, there would be room for many more beads.

"I'm sorry," she whispered. She took the poppet out of her pocket. "Do you want your luck back?"

I gently pushed her hand away. "Your brother is right. You're like us and you can't live off kindness. Keep the poppet."

Though I hoped the luck was for her and not for her brother.

The houses on East Street were not like the ones on the square. They were narrower and squashed together. If there was a Southwark in Southampton, this was it. The roaming dogs belonged to no one, just like the Southwark ones and, just like in Southwark, they were happy to leave their mess everywhere. They shared the streets with geese. I have always been more afraid of geese than dogs.

Some of the houses looked ready to tumble down, but Widow Primmer's house was solid, with tall, twisted chimneys and a slate roof. Widow Primmer reminded me of her house, tall and thin, and she had red curls corkscrewing out of her bonnet. She was quick to smile and really did seem happy to have us there. Her daughter, Claire, had been sick as a baby and had never fully recovered. Her head was shaved to keep her brain cool and she cried and shouted often. Widow Primmer said that she had to be with Claire almost every minute, because Claire didn't understand danger. When Widow Primmer was busy, Claire had to be confined to her chamber.

Mama and I were to make sure Claire was washed and in clean clothes, ate what was served to her and that her chamber pot was emptied. The first time Widow Primmer unlocked Claire's door, the chamber pot shot through the air towards us, scattering its contents across the floor. Mama whispered that Claire should be recruited to stand on the gatehouse by the quay to defend the town against the French. Claire could do more damage than any musket.

Emptying the chamber pot was the easiest task. Nobody asked Claire what food she liked or when she wanted to eat it or what clothes she wanted to wear, or if indeed she would prefer to have hair or not. I wasn't surprised she was angry. Mama was good at soothing her. She said that she understood how Claire must feel.

We settled into our new life easily, too easily. Every day I tried to tell Mama about the beads. Every day I'd clear my throat and feel the words bubble in my mouth, but then pop before I could say them. I did try and remind her about finding Jacques Francis, but she'd just laugh and tell me not to worry.

"We have months, Eve. Months!"

One week passed. Then another. One morning there was a knock at the door. Mama was with Claire, and Widow Primmer's hands were sticky with the dough she was kneading. It was strange. I had never opened a front door before. Mama and I were normally lower than the servants who opened the front door – that's if we lived somewhere with a door at all. I drew back the latch, twisted the key and pulled the door open, an inch at a time. Gina was standing there with Griffin by her side.

I went to hug Gina, but Griffin stepped between us.

"Good morning, Widow Primmer," he called past me. "Are you able to spare Eve this morning?"

I glanced back. "Don't you want me to scrub the pots, Mistress?"

"You can do that later," Widow Primmer said. "Go with Griffin, but collect some bacon on the way home."

Griffin pulled the door shut and nudged me down the steps. As I came down on to the cobbles, we disturbed two cats scavenging for scraps in the gutter. One of them, a scrappy grey thing with a dark blotch across its back, raised its head and looked at us. A fish head dangled from its mouth.

"The cats are getting bold," Griffin said. "Usually they stay hidden. Maybe they've come out to welcome you."

Gina glared at him. "Leave her alone."

He raised his hands. "I've done nothing to her."

Gina took my hand and tucked it through her arm. "We're leaving tomorrow and Griffin thought…" Another hard look towards her brother. "He thought that you may have forgotten your debt to him."

"To *us*," Griffin said. "Show her what's owed."

"I don't have to," Gina snapped back.

Griffin stepped towards her. "I said, show her!"

Gina glared at him. With her free hand, she drew the worsted bag out of her pocket. She didn't have to open it to show me how much fuller it was. She handed it to me. I could feel its weight in my palm. How many beads were in there now? I was too afraid to ask. I gave it back to her.

"Perhaps you need some assistance finding your diver," Griffin said. "As you don't seem to have enjoyed much success with your search so far."

"We've been settling in," I said.

"And now you should be settled."

"Do you know where he is?" I asked.

"No," Gina said. "But my brother's decided that we should take you to the places where you might find him."

If it wasn't for Griffin lurking behind us, I would have felt like a rich lady with my own escort showing me the sights of a new country. The places we lingered, though, were not those that rich people usually favoured. We carried on down East Street, out through the East Gate and across a bridge over a ditch. We came out on to common land next to a herd of cows. They ignored us. They were too busy eating.

"If your diver needs wood or peat for his fire," Griffin said, "you may find him here."

"There's a well too," Gina added.

"Yes," Griffin smirked. "Perhaps your diver has become a washerwoman."

Gina turned her back on him. "See over there? Those are orchards."

I nodded, though I knew that I would never recognize an apple tree unless there were apples on it.

They took me to Biddles Gate over by the quay. It was where boats were repaired and there was a crane hoisting barrels from a small vessel on to the wharf.

"There is sometimes work to be had here," Griffin said. "For those who like to be close to the water."

I didn't mention that Jacques Francis worked with an apothecary. Mama had been right: trust no one.

I followed them to the God's House Tower. We went through the gatehouse and looked down at the water working the mill beneath it.

"There are guns up on the roof," Gina said. I squinted up into the sunshine, but I couldn't see them.

"If your diver has a steady hand with a musket," Griffin said, "he could be there. If he is, make sure you find him soon."

"Why?"

"The tower holds the gunpowder store. Just one spark, and—" Griffin made an explosion sound. If a fire took hold, I wondered if Jacques Francis would dive off the battlements into the water below.

"You know Southampton well," I said to Gina.

"I was born here."

"And Griffin?"

"He was born in London. When his father died, Mama married my father. He was from here but had been working in the shipyards in Greenwich. There was too much sickness in London so they came back here and I was born. My granddad had been a porter, taking the cargo between the merchants and the harbour. By the time he died, he was bent double like a cartwheel. Even still, my father became a porter too, but the harbours were quieter then. Soon there was little for him to do. He could claim any goods he found in the street, but where there's no money, there's nothing to take."

"What did he do?" I asked.

"He went back to London."

"Was that better?"

Gina shrugged. "We don't know. We never heard from him again. He left no money for us and Mama couldn't marry anyone else because we had no word that my father was dead."

"Where's your mama now?" I asked.

"In the cemetery." She took my arm again, gripping it tighter than before.

We walked past the Watergate, the way to the main wharf, and then back along English Street.

"There's one last place to look," Griffin said.

Gina pulled me closer to her. "We don't have to."

We had arrived by the big stone gate that was the main entrance to Southampton. I now know that it was called the Bargate. I hadn't noticed the pillories before, perhaps because they had been empty. Of course, it wasn't the first time I'd ever seen pillories. No one can live in Southwark and not meet someone who'd spent time in them.

Today it was a woman in them. A small crowd had gathered around her, laughing and shouting insults. She was perhaps the same age as my mother. Her bonnet had been lost and her hair was loose and wild about her neck. Then I saw it. Of course, I knew that it happened, and I must have seen it before, but I'd always looked away without thinking. This time I could clearly see that the woman's ear had been nailed to the pillory post. I'd seen men and women in Southwark who were missing an ear, sometimes two. They lost their whole ear when the sheriff didn't want to waste time unpicking the nail so used a sword to free them instead. A piece of paper was stuck to her forehead. This would have told me her crime – if I'd known how to read it.

An apple core hit her cheek. The woman's eyes swivelled to seek out who had thrown it. She opened her mouth and let out a string of blasphemy so strong that my mouth dropped open in shock.

Griffin was behind me. He bent low to make sure I didn't miss his words.

"Danger is everywhere, Eve. I want you to know that."

A man close to the prisoner hurled the dregs from his tankard. The slops hit the cobbles just in front of her, and a little splashed up on to her hem. Her dress was torn and stained. One of her feet was wrapped in wool, the other jammed into a tight leather pump that sagged at the seams.

"She's a thief," Griffin said. "And a beggar. The councillors here are quite lenient and the crowd is tame. Perhaps they know her. They are harsher to strangers. I've heard that they gather the dung and the slops left over from the fish market, then search their pantries for rotting cheese and meat. They bring the stinking mess to the square, ready for the spectacle."

I shivered. The same was true in London. Stones were forbidden, but they were hidden in rotting food and rags.

I turned to look him in the eye. "Mama and I are not beggars. We haven't done anything wrong. There's no reason for us to be in the pillories."

"Is that so? What do the townspeople know of you, Eve? What do you think they will believe about you? You're foreigners."

"I know we're foreigners," I said. "But we're lodging with Widow Primmer. We're not begging or sleeping on the streets. She can vouch for us."

"You know well that there are many reasons why

women end up in the pillories. If you've committed a crime, even Widow Primmer can't save you."

He nodded his head towards the pillories. I didn't want to look at them again.

"Sometimes it's a mother who has a child without a husband," he said.

Mama had a husband. She told me about him. He was called Joseph Cartwright and she met him soon after arriving in London. He died when I was a baby and was buried in a pauper's grave with no possessions to bequeath to her.

"Do you and your mother attend church, Eve?"

"Church?"

Some Sundays we attended, some we did not. Mama slept through the sermon and didn't know the words to the hymns.

"There's a prison below the Bargate," Griffin said. "It's where they keep the people who don't attend and those who stick to the old faith. Perhaps the townsfolk will suspect that your mother still takes mass as a Catholic. Can you prove that she doesn't?"

The woman had stopped shouting. Her eyes drooped like she was trying to stop herself falling asleep. Her head jerked a little. If she slumped forward, she would lose her ear.

"I have to return home," I said.

I freed my arm from Gina's and tried to push past Griffin. He held my shoulder.

"There's one last thing you should know."

"Don't!" Gina shouted.

"I would be doing Eve a disservice if I didn't warn her, Gina." His pale-grey eyes reminded me of ashes. "There's a special whipping post for flogging witches."

"My mother is not a witch!"

"I'm not saying that she is, but the townspeople will be watching. Claire has been the same way for many years. If she improves … if she worsens … that would be witchcraft."

"My mother is not a witch!"

"There were two cats at your mother's door today—"

"That does not make her a witch!" My voice was louder.

"Who knows what the townspeople will think…"

A scream sounded from the pillories. The woman was being released. A man was fussing round her head. I hoped that he was trying to extract the nail rather than taking the quick way. I turned and walked away. I wanted to run, back to East Street and back to my mother. I wanted to feel her apron against my cheek and her fingers in my hair. But I wouldn't run, I would walk. Griffin needed to understand – we were strong.

THE PEARL EARRING

February was passing. Sunrise came earlier and sunset later. I had more time to search the town. I grew to know every crossroads and corner as well as I had done in Southwark. My favourite place was the Watergate. I'd sit on the steps watching the sailors preparing for high tide. Sometimes I'd imagine my mother breaking the surface of the water with a gold chain around her neck. She'd hand me a rope tied to a sack of gold that I'd help her lift out of the water. One day as I sat dreaming, I saw a face as brown as mine. My heart beat so hard, it nearly made the waves move. I started to rise, then I saw clearly that it was a sailor, a younger man with long hair and the start of a beard. Our eyes met, we smiled at each other and then he went about his business. Sometimes I'd walk round by the East Gate, though I was always more careful there. The houses were patched together, leaning against the wall. A strong storm would easily blow them away. Cows and pigs wandered between the homes, and it seemed to me that those creatures weren't the only ones leaving their waste along the pathways.

I was just coming from Biddles Gate when I spotted him. I had been watching the crane load chests on to a ship. The men working the treadmill had been singing a song I recognized from Bankside. The man I spotted was walking along the quay, hugging close to the wall. I would have missed him if he hadn't glanced up. Gun ports ran across the top of the ramparts and Widow Primmer had told me that once an explosion there had killed a man and left several injured. *Everybody* looked up at the guns when they walked by. As his face tipped up, I was looking down and I knew straight away that it was him – the man from the inn. He was wearing the same high-crowned cap, and I wasn't sure, but I thought I spotted a small, cream pearl earring. He saw me, his eyes widened and then he looked away. He spun round and strode off.

No! He couldn't disappear again! I jumped up and stumbled down the slippery stairs on to the quay. He *had* disappeared. A group of fishermen were scraping pitch over their boats by the shore.

I stopped in front of them. "Excuse me, sirs!"

They looked up.

"The man—" I pointed to the empty space where

he had been. "Do you know him?"

"I see no man," one of them laughed. He was young, not too many years older than me and trying to grow a beard. "Are you looking for a ghost?"

"He walked past here a moment ago," I said. "He has dark skin, like mine."

"I've seen him about." This was from an older fisherman. He scratched his ear. "I think he's waiting for cargo."

"Do you know where he lives?" I asked him.

The fisherman frowned. "Why does that interest a child?" Then he laughed. "Of course, I see it! The family resemblance!" He nudged the younger one. "Don't you see it?"

Family resemblance? Oh, they thought he was my father! We looked nothing alike, but…

"I need to find him." I bowed my head and tried to look meek. "My mother sent me from Southwark to fetch him back."

"He used to lodge with Nicholas Balcombe," the older fisherman said. "At the apothecary shop on French Street. I've heard old man Balcombe isn't coming back from London, but you could try there."

They turned back to their work, joking about my "abandoned" mother. French Street was back near the Watergate. I had to be quick if I was to catch him.

*

He was standing in the street by the closed door of
the apothecary shop, scraping mud from his boot. I
waited behind him, hoping he would turn around.
I'm surprised my thumping heart didn't alert him. He
carried on scraping his boots though they seemed clean
to me.

"Sir," I said.

Scrape, scrape.

"Please hear me, sir."

He turned around. I thought there would be
anger on his face, but it was just weariness. "Are you
following me?"

"No, sir."

He raised his eyebrows. "Is it just coincidence that I
saw you in the inn and then on the rampart? And now
you appear outside my lodgings?"

What could I say? Did I tell him that I thought he
could lead us to treasure? Did I lie? Mama had said *trust
no one*, because everybody lied. Perhaps he was tired of
lies too.

I said, "My mother can dive deep. She learned it
in the country where she was born, before she was
brought here."

Scrape, scrape. "Why should this interest me?"

"I thought perhaps you were Master Jacques Francis, the diver."

He surveyed me without blinking. It made me look away and stop talking.

"My name is Anthony," he said. He inserted his key into the door, pushed it open and banged it shut in my face.

I stood there for a moment, my nose touching the wood. Suddenly, my anger was so bright I could almost see it. It was like the fireworks that sometimes glitter in the sky on the other side of the Thames. We would see an explosion of light then a big bang. My fury was like that, bursting behind my eyes then thundering through my head. Mama and I, we did not have easy lives. People like us died in the streets from the cold or from hunger or from burning fever or swelling. But we weren't dead yet. We'd been given a chance to improve our situation and this rude man, who could so easily help us, had slammed a door in my face.

I hammered on the door and waited. Nothing. I thumped it so hard, I felt the wood tremble.

"If you don't let me in," I shouted, "I'll sit here until nightfall."

I must have made a strange sight, sitting on the doorstep of a closed apothecary shop. I think every dog in Southampton came up to sniff me, and a stray pig too. As evening fell, a sharp breeze knifed off the sea. I could hear merriment from a tavern across the street and could smell – was that frying fish? Yes, frying fish. My stomach gurgled. Mama would be worried about me, but I couldn't leave, not after all this time. I wondered if *Master Anthony* was enjoying a hearty meal in front of a roaring fire.

I stood up and kicked the door. "I'm still here!"

Nothing. Did he have a back way out? Was he long gone? No, there was a flicker of a candle behind the glass. I stretched up to tap the window, then pulled my hand back. If he hadn't answered when I'd kicked the door, a mere tap wouldn't bother him. I had to make sure he really heard me. There was pebble in my pocket. I'd found it down by the quay and picked it up because it was the shape of an arrowhead. I knocked it hard against the glass. Once. Just once. The glass cracked, fell apart and fell inwards. It was only a small pane, but there was a reason why only rich people had glass windows. Glass was *very* expensive. I stepped back, the pebble still in my hand. I could run. I *should* run. Right now!

The door flew open. The man was standing there. He looked over my head, up and down the street, as if he'd expected that someone grown had done the damage. Then he looked down and saw me. He pointed to the hole where the glass had been.

"Was that you?"

I nodded. Just like the fireworks, my fury had burned bright then disappeared. The anger must have been keeping me warm too, because now I felt the coldness of the evening. The wind felt like it wanted to slice my skin away. I shivered.

"Come inside," he said. "Warm yourself up while you explain how you're going to fix the window."

The front room was the shop. Three candles burned on the counter and their flames reflected off the shelves of glass bottles. I could just make out the shards of glass from the window on the floor. I crouched over them, trying to brush them together with my hands. I wasn't sure what I intended to do with them.

He bent over me. The flame flickered in his eyes. "Leave it, before you cut yourself."

He straightened up and I followed him into a back room. There was little in there apart from a table, a wooden chair tucked under it and another chair drawn close to a small fire. A basket of kindling and small logs sat in a basket at the side of the hearth.

He pointed to the chair. "Sit there."

The chair was warm from the fire. I reached down, grasping the arms to try and warm my palms. He prodded the fire with a poker, but the flames seemed to become even smaller. I thought it needed more kindling, but my teeth were chattering too much to tell him. I stretched my feet out towards what little heat there was and my toes started to uncurl.

"I'm sorry," I said.

"*Sorry* does not pay for glass," he replied.

"I'll … I'll pay."

"Do you have the money to pay?"

"I … I would like to earn money."

"I have no means to employ you."

He threw a handful of kindling into the fire. It flared up and he quickly laid a log on top of it. For a moment I wondered if he'd collected his wood from the common land. Had he been there and I'd missed him? I'd asked some of the women washing their linen on Houndwell if they knew of him. They hadn't.

I said, "You have the means to help Mama and me make our fortune."

"You're mistaken."

"Mama and I are poor," I said. "We've lived in more places than I can name. Sometimes we have nowhere to sleep at all."

"Do you have a roof over your heads now?"

"Yes. But it won't be for ever. Mama didn't ask to come to England, but she still has to suffer hardships."

He drew the other chair from beneath the table and placed it across from me. "None of us ask to be here," he said. "But once that choice has been made for us, we have to make the best of it."

"That's what Mama wants to do."

"Perhaps so, but I can't help you or your Mama."

He was staring into the fire. He reached forward and lifted the burning log with the poker. Flames roared under it, then up around it as if the fire was swallowing it whole. A blast of heat hit my face. The earlier cold made it feel even hotter. He let the log drop again.

"Mama was born on an island far away," I said. "She told me they called it Mozambique."

She had told me how she'd lived in a small house with a roof made from palm leaves. She'd had to draw palm leaves for me as we didn't have palm trees in Southwark. Some of the leaves were so big, she'd said, she could wrap me up in them. The Portuguese had been there for as long as she could remember, and she could speak Portuguese as well as her own language of Swahili. Now she only spoke Portuguese when she was sinking and her own language never, except for calling me *mpendwa*. When she'd first seen the Tower of London, it had made her think of the big stone fort that she'd seen the Portuguese starting to build on one side of her island.

"Mama said she was a child when she was taken," I said.

He still didn't speak.

"Her island was surrounded by rocks and she would swim out to them with her older brothers. One morning, she swam back to shore by herself. That's when she was stolen. She says that she hopes her brother told their mother that she had drowned. She didn't want to imagine her mother standing by the shore hoping she would return. She won't talk about her journey, though she once told me she was put on a boat with a chain around her neck, then taken to a market square in Lisbon in Portugal and sold. After that she was taken to a city built on water."

"I know it," he said.

I waited. I'd learned that it was best to let Mama tell her stories in her own time, especially as she often struggled to find words that I would understand.

"The city is called Venice. I spent many years there. It was not where I wanted to be, but I didn't suffer like some. I..." He gave me a sideways look. "I had skills they found useful."

"My mama was a maid," I said. "She has a scar across her back from where her mistress poured hot wax across her."

The fire flared and crackled. I would have to return

soon. Mama would be starting to worry.

"Are you … are you Jacques Francis?" I asked.

"I've had many names. That was one of them. But it does you no good to know that. I still cannot help you."

"They say—"

"I am old. I know what they say. Would I be an apothecary's errand boy if it was true? I would be living the life of a rich man surrounded by gold."

I couldn't see his face to read his expression.

"Is there no treasure at all?" I asked.

"I did not say that there was no treasure. There are plenty of secrets below those waters and some of those secrets may be gold, but I would not risk my life to find them."

"But you risked your life for others."

"And I made a decision that I would never do it again."

"You wouldn't have to. All you'd have to do is tell Mama where to dive. That's all."

"And even if she came back with bags of gold, do you think they would let her keep it? Do you think your mother's life would be easier? If she is happy now, let her stay happy."

She was only happy because she knew nothing about Griffin's bag of beads. Soon there would be so many the drawstring would not pull tight. Then what?

I thought of the woman in the pillories, her hem damp with slops and her ear nailed to the post. I had looked out for her in the town since then, but perhaps she had gone elsewhere.

Jacques Francis stood up. He went back into the shop and I heard the sound of a chest opening and closing. He came back with a cloak draped over his arm.

"Put this on as best as you can."

I slid off the chair and tied the cloak around my neck. It brushed the floor. He opened the door and the cold pushed past him into the back room. I wrapped the cloak tight around me. He was already striding away. I ran after him.

"Where are we going?"

He didn't answer. We were the evening's entertainment for many in Southampton that night, especially me trotting along, trying not to trip over the cloak or let it drag in the dirt. We turned into St Michael's Square. The church was dark and empty, the traders long gone. Lanterns flickered in the windows of the merchants' houses surrounding us.

Jacques Francis raised his arms. "This is where the Venetian tried to sell me."

Sell him? I thought of conger eels on the fishmongers' slabs and bundles of dented spoons or poppets and pallets piled with old clothes. There were markets that sold chickens, horses and cows. Those were the markets I knew. But I also knew that there were other markets that sold people. But Jacques Francis was a diver, the best. He couldn't be a sl— I hated even thinking the word.

"Was he was seeking payment for your services?" I asked.

"For my services?" His voice lowered. "No, he was seeking payment for me. In Venice and other countries, people like me and your mother are bought and sold like a wool blanket. Except, merchants care for their blankets better than their slaves."

Mama had said that in Portugal, slaves were worked until they dropped dead. They were owned like a horse, but fed less.

"Mama said that there is no slavery in England. Isn't Southampton in England?"

"Yes, Southampton is in England, but there are Englishmen on Portuguese soil who own slaves. Perhaps that's why that rogue, Corsi, stood here as bold as the moon above us and offered me for sale to the highest bidder."

"Did anyone bid?" I clapped my hand over my mouth. That was a question I should have kept inside.

Jacques Francis didn't answer. I looked up at the moon. It was definitely brighter without London's smoke. I wished it would shine some light into my head and help me see what I was supposed to do next. He leaned forward. He reminded me of the archers practising on the salt marsh. When they pull back their bow, it seems that their whole body, not just their arms, are bent towards making that arrow hit its mark.

He said, "Can you hear it?"

I could hear the bagpipes from a tavern in a neighbouring street and singing coming from down by the waterfront.

"Hear what, sir?" I said.

He shook his head. "I think it's only me who hears it. So many men were lost beneath the water that sometimes I wonder if they're calling to me. When we dived for the *Mary Rose*, I went into the water with my head full of pewter plate, gold coins and my rewards for bringing up the king's guns, but all I saw at first were the bones. We had to reach between them to take what we could find. Even in the men's death, there was no rest. Sometimes, a mother or wife would come up to us as we disembarked. They wanted to know if their son or husband was at peace. But people don't care about boys and men when there's tin and lead and cannon to find."

I imagined the sea sweeping back like a curtain to show the bare bed and the wrecks of boats and everything in them. The *Mary Rose* was only one ship. Standing there, in the cold moonlit square, with the smell of pitch and the scream of a gull, and the river not far away, my stomach heaved as if it was filling with water. I could feel the suck of the river in and out of my ears and then my face, head and my whole body was submerged. I had forgotten about the things floating in the Thames, brushing my cheeks, brushing against my arms and wrapping around my ankles. Then I remembered the voices, asking me my story.

"You learn not to look," he said. "You've come from London?"

"We live in Southwark."

"Then you've seen death."

It was everywhere in our streets. Mama had once nursed a young woman who died as her baby was being born. Mama had seen me peering round the door and closed it gently. Last winter, I had seen a young man who had frozen to death in a butcher's doorway.

"I would feel the dead's presence," he said, "as I was scavenging for the merchants' riches. I was the best diver of all of them. The sea around my island had been my first home. It was a strong, wild sea that beat against our shore. Boats tried to land and soon our waters were full of their cracked hulls. My friends and I used to dive among the wrecks looking for treasure. The only treasure we ever found was fish hooks and coins that were no use to us."

He looked up at the moon. "They stole us at night. Our island was already not our own, but at first they didn't bother us. I wonder now if they were watching us, thinking about how much money we could bring them. First, they made me bring up oysters for pearls. When there were no more oysters, I was taken to Portugal and handed over to Corsi in Lisbon. He baptized me and gave me my new name."

I wanted to ask him what his name had been before. I had asked Mama that too, but she would never answer me. It was like she saved that little bit of her old life just for herself.

"There were three of us," he said. "From what, in these countries, they call Africa. Me, I was the youngest. Then there was George Blacke, a short man with a chest like a wine barrel. I think it held more breath than anyone else's, because he could dive for the longest. John Iko was little more than a child, tall and thin, like he'd been turned on the rack. He drank more beer than me and George put together."

"Where are they now?"

"To survive, we must scatter. When they believed I brought shame on them, all my friends disappeared."

He started walking again, tracing the perimeter of

the square. He was still talking. I trotted along beside him.

"I was the one Corsi said he trusted the most, the one who went the deepest." He rubbed his ears. "Diving isn't just a matter of holding your breath. You must know how to balance the weight of the water. You cannot just drop down there like a stone and carry on about your business. You have to learn how to see in those dark depths. You have to feel with your fingers, to understand what you are touching and not flinch away. Your ears burn, deep inside. Your face feels like an eagle has gripped it with hungry claws."

I touched my own ears. Would that have happened to me if I'd carried on to the bottom of the Thames?

We stopped walking. I thought he was going to go round again, but he turned back towards French Street.

"I was the best," he said. "And even after Corsi tried to sell me, I still was loyal. I testified in a court of law in London that Corsi had not stolen tin from another merchant. I said that the tin was found far away by the rocks. My English wasn't good then. I had to trust the wine merchant to interpret correctly. Do you know what they called me?"

"No, sir."

"Infidel," he said. "That was their name for me. They said that because I was born in a different land, I was a slave and a liar.

"When I dived," he continued, "I was filled with calmness. I would feel my heart beating. I would understand how much air to hold inside me and how much to release." He held his fingers near his eyes. "I would feel the water pressing me as if I was caught between two heavy stones, but I stayed calm, because if I didn't, I would die. But afterwards, after those merchants ganged together to question my word, I became angry. I tried one more dive, but my breath wanted to burst out of me. For the first time since I was a child, blood poured out of my nose and my ears felt as if they had been pierced with heated pins."

"Are you still angry?" I asked.

"Yes. Now go to your mother. She will be worried."

A GOLD COIN ON THE COMMON

Mama is beautiful. She is not beautiful like the rich ladies in their ruffs and furs and jewels, though she would be so much more beautiful than them if she ever had a chance to wear pearls and silk. She has brown skin, warm beneath the dust and dirt of our lives. She has marks from the smallpox and each scar reminds me that I am lucky to have her alive. Her eyes are almost the same colour as her skin, and her lashes are black and long. They twitch in her sleep like they can hear music and are longing to dance. Her hair, when it's free from her coif cap, is thick and tied in one or two plaits.

As March tipped into April, I spent every moment I could with her. I'd be tidying Claire's chamber while Mama helped Claire eat, or I'd be sitting with Claire on her bed as Mama told us stories or sang us songs in her own language. I'd stand side by side with Mama as we chopped vegetables and I'd help her sweep away the old rushes on the floor and lay down new ones. I hurt if I couldn't see her because I knew that each day a new bead would drop into Griffin's bag. I wondered how often he counted them and smiled at the fortune he saw coming his way. Then I'd remember the woman in the pillories. Her face would fade away and it would be Mama's instead.

I still walked around the town but I kept my head down. Folks had always glanced at Mama and me wherever we went, although less so in Southwark, where all manner of people made their home. Now I did not want to meet anyone's eye. Mama and I were foreigners. Did they think badly of us? The day before, I had seen two young women coming towards me. Servants, I'd thought. They'd turned to each other and one whispered. Did they believe I was a witch about to curse them? Did the priest in St Lawrence's Church see me pass by and wonder why I hadn't attended service on Sunday? Did he think Mama had been baptized a Catholic and wonder if she'd converted? Did he question whether I'd been baptized at all? The path that Mama and I were treading felt so delicate.

Sometimes I would see Jacques Francis down by the wharf. We would nod to each other, but we wouldn't speak. He would never change his mind, I knew that now. But, I had to remind myself, I was an adventurer. Adventures always went wrong before they ended well. It just meant making a different plan. One day I was sitting by Biddles Gate trying to work out what that plan could be when a voice called up to me.

"You!"

I looked down. It was the young fisherman who'd been there the day I first saw Jacques Francis. He was standing by an upturned boat. He rubbed his hands together.

"I'm still seeing your *dada* about," he said. "Doesn't he want to go back with you?"

"He's not my father."

The fisherman rubbed his hands again. His palms were so black with pitch, I was surprised they didn't stick together.

"That's a pity. I heard he's got a room full of gold." He started to climb the steps towards me. "They say he goes out into the river at night and doesn't need a lantern because he can see in the dark. He swims right out to where the treasure is and when we're all sleeping, he picks it off the bottom of the river and takes it home for himself."

The fisherman's head was now level with mine. His cheek was streaked with black and there was a lump of pitch knotted in his hair.

"There's a richer harvest than eels in that water," he said. "I'd take a boat and look myself, if I could swim. But if I tried, I'd just be another load of bones sitting on the river bed." He smiled at me. His teeth looked like he'd been rubbing pitch on them too. "But if someone else could swim, I'd show them where all the gold was and we could share the bounty."

I gave him a sideways look. This was just another sailors' tale.

"I suppose you know where the boat went down," I said.

"Yes," he said. "Of course I know."

"The *Sancta Maria and Sanctus Edwardus*?"

He nodded hard. "Yes. That one."

"How do you know?"

"Everyone does. Do you want me to show you?"

"I..."

You're an adventurer, Eve. You need a plan.

"I can't swim, but I know someone who can. If there really is treasure, they might be able to help."

"Well, how about you come back this evening and bring them with you?"

This evening? Mama would never come out with me. I'd even stopped reminding her about her promise to George Symons. She said she'd tell him the truth when he came to Southampton, that there was no treasure. But how did she know when she hadn't even tried to look?

"She won't be able to come this evening," I said.

"How about you? I can show you where it is."

If I went with him, I could find out the exact spot where Mama had to dive. Maybe the fisherman would help me find out how deep it was too, so she'd be able to prepare herself. We didn't need Jacques Francis after all. We could make our fortune by ourselves. Except...

"How big is your boat?" I asked.

He waved his hand towards the quay. "It's a fishing boat."

It was even smaller than a wherry. The river here was calm, though, and there were no arches for it to rush through. Could I take a boat out into the river at night to find treasure? That would be a real adventure! But what if I couldn't do it? What if I took one step into the boat and had to jump back on to the shore?

"I'm ... not sure. I don't really like boats."

He smiled again. "No matter. If you can't see where we found the gold, I can still show you some, to prove I'm not lying."

"You've already found gold?"

How could he be rich and still be a fisherman? He was wearing patched breeches and stockings and a smock that was stiff with dirt.

"Just a few coins. They came up in my net. That's how I know it's there."

Real, actual treasure! What if I could take some and show Mama? Then she'd *have* to agree to dive.

"When can I see it?" I asked.

The fisherman thought. "We need to be away from prying eyes. There are enough rumours already. We don't want others knowing they're true. I've also got to look after myself. I can't take you to the place where I keep it, in case you tell other people."

"I won't tell other people." Apart from Mama, of course. "Would I be able to borrow one of your coins?"

"Borrow my coins..." He frowned. "I don't think I could allow that."

"It's just ... just so I can show the person who can help us get the rest of it. They might not believe me unless I show them."

"I understand. Can I trust you?"

"Yes!"

"How about you meet me on the salt marsh, right by the bowling green? I'll bring some coins and maybe I'll let you take one away."

"Thank you! When shall I be there?"

"I have to finish with the boat then go and collect my coin. Then I'll be there."

I ran home. Would I tell Mama where I was going?

Once I was sure there was treasure, we'd go out together and maybe the picture I'd seen in my head would be true – Mama rising from the water with gold glittering around her neck.

As I opened Widow Primmer's door, a cat shot out from inside. It stood by the doorway across the street. It was the grey one with the dark blotch on its back. He'd grown fat in the last month. I wasn't sure if it was because of the scraps Mama fed him or the rats he hunted down in the yard. He cocked his head and blinked at me as if he knew my secrets.

Inside, Mama was whisking a pot. The smell of spices wafted towards me. She tipped the pot so I could see inside. There were yellow bits that looked eggy and white liquid that could be milk or cream. I wasn't sure about the dark brew it was all floating in. I sniffed again.

"Is that wine?" I asked.

"I'm making posset," Mama said. "Claire was up and wandering the room last night. I hope it might calm her. There may be some extra left over if you would like it."

"I didn't know you could make posset," I said.

Mama stared at the mess in the pot. "I'm not sure I can either." She held up the spoon. Egg lumps plopped back into the pan. "Like to taste it?"

I wiped my finger across the spoon then into my mouth. Mama had used a lot of honey. That was a good thing and it almost made me forget the chewy egg bits.

"Where's Widow Primmer?" I asked.

"Visiting some friends." Mama laughed. "Now we're here to care for Claire, she can do as she wishes." Mama poured the posset into a cup. A few egg lumps dropped in as well. "She said that we can stay as long as we like if we can find employment. Your poppet really did bring us luck!" She smiled, then stared into the cup. "I think I'd better strain this." She took the sieve from the shelf and drained the posset back into the pan, then once more into the cup.

"That's better," Mama said.

"Shall I come up with you?" I asked her.

"No, Claire is calmer when it's just me."

"Will you be long?"

"It depends if she wants to talk a while. Are you jealous?"

"No, Mama. I just … it's just we told George Symons we'd find the gold. He'll be here soon, won't he?"

Mama held up the pot. "We already have treasure. I'm queen of the kitchen and we are dry and warm with a roof over our head. Do we need more?"

Yes, Mama. There is a boy with a bag full of brown beads

and the bag is getting heavier and fuller. He only has to open his mouth and they will come for you.

But how could I tell her this when I knew that her happiness could crack any time?

I said, "This is good for now, Mama, but it might not be for ever."

"Nothing is for ever, Eve. But do we want to test God's patience and be greedy with our luck?" She wrapped a cloth round the hot cup and took a spoon from a jar. "Instead of questioning our destiny, please go and scour the pots. I promised the widow they would be done by the time she returned."

Perhaps Mama was right. Perhaps luck flowed through our lives like water through the conduits. If you tried to draw more than your fair share of water, there'd be a washerwoman standing behind you ready to poke you hard in the back and toss you aside. We didn't want our luck to turn on us. But – what if there was a real chance of something better?

I went out into the yard. A stack of plates and pots was waiting to be scoured. These weren't just from yesterday. Mama and the widow must have been saving them for a while. I picked up a large, misshapen pot. The bottom was so burnt it looked like the widow had been making charcoal in it. A couple of plates were crusted with gravy so old it was almost part of the design. How was I going to get this off? Back in Southwark, I'd seen Mama use sand or horsetail she'd picked from the fields by Broadwall. I poked around the yard and checked in the kitchen. I could see neither sand nor horsetail.

Where could I find horsetail? I laughed to myself. On the common, of course! I was sure I'd seen goats nibbling it there. And I could go down on to the mudflats to get sand and small stones to bring back for the hard scrubbing. I wouldn't even have to lie to Mama about where I was going. I'd hide my treasure underneath it all on my way home too. I took a pitcher and a knife from the kitchen shelf and went back out.

I walked outside the town walls, along the orchard lane. Down here the walls stretched up high above me. I couldn't imagine anyone breaking through, especially as they'd filled the ditch alongside the walls with holly and bramble. I had never wanted to live inside London's walls. London was so busy, it wanted to burst out from behind the stones. For Mama though, I think the walls and gates and watchmen made her feel safer. Soon, we would have enough money for her to have her own house with her own door with as many bolts and latches as she wished.

I reached the end of the orchard and skirted around the bowling green. I spotted a clump of horsetail, took my knife out of the pitcher and bent towards them. A ladycow beetle climbed a stalk as if to greet me. I counted seven black spots like holes on its red shell. Was seven a lucky number? As I reached out my hand, its shell clicked open and its wings emerged. As it landed on my finger, my world went dark and I stopped breathing.

A SPLASH IN THE DARK

It was a sack that suffocated me this time, not water. The roughness rubbed against my skin. As I tried to breathe, my nose was filled with the smell of rotting hay. My hands were yanked behind my back and rope tightened around my wrists, the fibres cutting into my skin. They'd soon be speckled with my blood.

I felt the warmth of the man next to my face before I heard his voice. "Don't try to run away. I know your mama is with Widow Primmer's daughter. If you run, my friends will know what to do."

His accent wasn't like the townsfolk's. It wasn't from Southwark or even London, but I was sure I'd heard voices like his before. I tried to speak but my mouth was filled with sack and I thought I would choke.

"If you cry out," the voice said, "we will go to the house and we will scatter the daughter's blood and make sure your mama takes the blame."

"Hurry up! We can't stay here!" This was a different voice, a local one. A voice that I'd heard earlier. The voice that told me to meet him here to see treasure. *Trust no one*, Mama had said. *TRUST NO ONE!* Why had I forgotten?

"Have you ever seen a hanging?" the stranger's voice said. I could smell his dank breath through the threads of the sack. "A hanging hurts. It hurts for a long, long time before you die because they want to show all the people watching that it hurts. If you're lucky, a friend will pull on your legs to make it quicker. I don't think your mother's got friends. Will you step up to the gallows and help her die?"

"We have to go, Antonio! I told you, they don't allow this in England."

"So, you have to be quiet, Eve. You must not run. You must not shout, because there will be no mercy when the noose is around your mother's neck."

The shaking started in my shoulders and spread across my chest, out towards my arms and fingers and down to my toes. I tried to talk, to ask them what they wanted. Did they think I was going to steal their treasure? It didn't matter! I didn't want it. They didn't have to tie me up and threaten Mama. I wanted to say all this but I was shaking too hard.

"Let's get her to the house," the fisherman said. "And don't forget the price we agreed." A finger poked my back. "You want to know where the treasure is? It's not in the water. It's right here. You're going to get me a good price."

That's when I understood. I was human treasure. I was going to be sold.

"Let's go!" The fisherman's fingers pressed into the sack until they found my ear. I felt the fisherman's cheek graze the sack.

"Listen carefully. Antonio's told you what's going to happen if you get it wrong. I'm going to take off this sack, right? You're not going to scream or shout or anything like that. Then I'm going to untie your arms. You keep them as if they're still tied. We're going to walk out of here and we're going to look like we're all friends. You're not going to look left nor right. You're not going to smile or frown at no one. Do you understand me?"

My voice was crawling back. "Where are you taking me?"

The finger poked my back again, harder. "Did you hear what I said?"

"Yes," I whispered.

The sack was whipped off my head and I took a deep breath. The heavy air dropped into my stomach so hard I almost vomited. I made myself look at the men. One was definitely the fisherman from earlier.

He gave me a big grin. The other was older and wore a cracked leather jerkin over his doublet and a cap pulled low over his brow. A wooden scabbard hung around his neck. A handle poked out from it and, when he was sure I had seen it, he lifted it a little so I could see the metal of his dagger.

The fisherman held his hand to his throat and made a choking sound. "Don't forget what Antonio said. You don't want to see your mama dangling."

Antonio told me to get up. I hadn't realized that I was on the ground. I must have fallen into the grass when they'd pulled the sack over my head.

"Hurry up!" the fisherman hissed.

When I didn't move quickly enough, he yanked me up. "I'm going to untie your hands. If you try and hit me, even if it doesn't hurt…" He made the choking noise again. "You're going to carry your bowl like everything is normal, you understand?"

He handed me my pitcher. It didn't rattle. The knife was gone. I had to hug the pitcher to my chest as it felt too heavy for my soft fingers. My legs were still floppy but I stood still for a second, willing strength down into them. I swayed, but stayed upright.

"Walk!" Antonio said. That's when I recognized the accent. It was the same as the man from the boat that George Symons had arranged for us, the one that Mama had refused to travel with. *The Portuguese stole me from my family.* I should have listened to her. I should have known that we'd drawn all the luck we were allowed. I had been greedy.

I looked down at my feet. I had to make them move. I tilted forward until I staggered and my feet shifted to stop me falling again. Right foot, then left. Right, left. Right, left.

"Faster!" Antonio shouted.

Right, left. My back jerked, like there was a cog missing. I could hear their footsteps close behind me.

"You know the way to French Street?" the fisherman asked.

I nodded.

"Quicker! Remember we're right behind you."

French Street was where Jacques Francis lodged. We would walk right past the apothecary shop. Was there still a trickle of luck left? My feet stumbled over the rough paving stones. It was hard to see through the tears streaming down my cheeks. There was a chill in the air and it was still bright, but it wouldn't be long before the sky would start to dim. I saw the apothecary shop ahead. *Please, Jacques! Please be there!* We passed it. The door was firmly shut, the hole in the window filled with a wad of wool. I tried to glance sideways without moving my head. I heard laughter and the slow clunk of donkey hooves and the creak of cartwheels behind us. The fisherman called out a greeting, but there was nothing more.

No one would save me. I would be taken to a boat. I would be sold.

I thought of Mama smiling as she lifted the spoon from the pot of posset. If I was never going to see her again, I wanted my last thoughts of her to be good ones. My earliest memories were of her singing, when I was frightened or when I couldn't sleep. She would stroke my hair in time to her words. Or she'd sing when she was scouring pots or as we queued with our buckets for water. We even had a special song for when she was tugging the comb through my hair to dislodge the lice. She'd sing while we sat sewing by candlelight, when my fingers felt too numb to carry on but the work had to be completed by morning if we were to be paid. She rarely sang in English. She didn't know many English songs. I think she made songs up sometimes, but I didn't mind.

A tune came into my head, one I had heard her singing for as long as I could remember. I couldn't just hear her, I could almost smell the lavender sweete bag she carried in her apron to ward off diseases. I could almost see the buttercups she entwined round her thumb to speed the healing of a knife wound. The song was Mama herself.

I didn't know the meaning of the Portuguese words, but I knew the sounds and the tune. I started singing gently, but then as Mama became almost real beside me, my song grew in volume.

The fisherman cuffed my shoulder. "Stop that noise!"

"No," Antonio said. "Continue. I know that song. My mama sang it to my sister. This girl is a big treasure! She will make the rich ladies happy!"

I sang harder to drown out their voices until there was another poke in my back.

"Stop!" the fisherman hissed.

We were standing outside a merchant's house, beneath the overhang of the upper storey.

"Do you have the key?" Antonio asked.

The fisherman took one from the pocket of his breeches and passed it to Antonio.

"He needs it back before nightfall."

"We'll be gone by then," Antonio said.

Antonio went ahead of me, not to the front door, but down the steps to the vault. The fisherman stayed guard at the top while Antonio fiddled with the key then pushed open the door. I looked into the heavy darkness. I could just see the sloping curves of the ceiling before I was shoved in to the black and the door slammed shut behind me.

The darkness wrapped round me like a shroud. I felt the floor beneath my feet and knew that there was a ceiling over me, but beyond that, I couldn't work out where I was in the room, or even how big the room was. I placed my pitcher on the ground and reached out my hands, walking slowly ahead until my fingers touched a stone wall. I pressed my back against it and slid to the floor. We would be gone by nightfall, Antonio had said. *Long gone.* Far away from everybody I knew. I wouldn't wish this time away. For every moment I was still in Southampton, there was a chance that someone would miss me and search for me. Perhaps if I stayed still enough, I would hear them calling my name.

I drew my knees in and sat, unmoving. I could smell a faint hint of the wine that had been stored here, but I sensed that the vault was empty now apart from me – me and whatever was scurrying in the far corners. I hugged my knees tighter. Mama would realize I was gone. She would find me. I listened and I listened, but no one called my name.

I don't know how long I was there. I don't know if I slept or not, because the darkness was the same whether my eyes were closed or open. The twist of the key in the lock sounded as loud as thunder after the thick silence of the vault. The door opened and the lantern light almost blinded me. I jumped up.

"Mama!"

A harsh laugh. "I'm not your mama, but we can find her and take her with us if you want!"

Antonio came towards me and pulled me out of the vault. The fisherman was guarding the steps again, so when Antonio let go of me to lock the door, there was nowhere for me to run, even if my cold, numb legs would have let me. Antonio passed the key back up to the fisherman. I heard the fisherman laugh and say something, then a shadow moved away from him.

"That was the easiest sixpence he ever earned," the fisherman said. "Just for the loan of a key. I hope I get my money back, Antonio."

"Once she's on the ship, you'll have your payment as we agreed." Antonio held up his lantern so I could see the impatience on his face. "Time to walk. And walk fast!"

I knew the path we were taking down French Street and on to the quay. I should scream now. I had nothing to lose. If the ship was already waiting, they had no time to hurt Mama. I took a deep breath.

"Hel—" A hand clapped across my mouth. The stink of pitch filled my nostrils.

"I thought you wanted your mama safe," the fisherman whispered in my ear. "For sixpence, Master Geoffrey's butler will loan me a key to his vault. There are desperate men in this town who will take my money to do far worse. Your mama will not be safe until Antonio's boat leaves these waters."

The quay was deserted. I looked back towards the ramparts crowning the wall and wondered about the guns and archers who defended the town. Was there no one looking down who could defend me? Would they see the splashes of light from our lanterns and wonder who we were? They'd probably just think we were sailors returning from a good meal in a tavern. A ship was anchored further out in the river. That must be where we were heading. The journey there would not be long. My time had run out.

The fisherman walked ahead of me, Antonio behind. The steps down to the quay were slippery with seaweed and I stumbled. Antonio muttered something about not damaging the goods and held my shoulders. Their rowing boat was moored near the steps and Antonio guided me towards it. A thin length of rope was coiled across its seats.

The fisherman saw me looking.

"I can't have you swimming back to shore," he said.

I wished I could. I wished I had made Mama show me how swimming was done. I wished I could slip over the side of the boat and float back to safety. Now the fear was already rising in me as the boat rocked on the tide. The fisherman jumped in. He wobbled a little but quickly regained his balance.

"Now you," Antonio said.

The tide made the boat veer away from the jetty.

"Steady it, will you?" the fisherman shouted.

Antonio yanked the mooring rope and pulled the boat closer.

"Hurry up!" he growled at me.

I took a step. The boat jerked at the rope and water lapped over the jetty on to my feet. Antonio swore, picked me up and dropped me into the puddle of water at the bottom of the boat. He unhooked the rope from its mooring and stepped in. He picked up an oar and pushed off from the jetty. The fisherman pulled me up to tie my wrists, testing his knot to make sure it was tight. I imagined my skin straining around my bones, but I wasn't going to give him the satisfaction of letting him know that it hurt.

"You row," Antonio said. "I'll guard her."

The fisherman grumbled about not being anyone's servant, but picked up the oars and started rowing. Each splash of wood into water was taking me further away from home. My fear became a solid lump inside my stomach. The River Test was not as rough as the Thames, but it was hard to forget how small our boat was and how wide and deep the water. The waves rocked us. The motion of the oars rocked us. The growing breeze blowing in from the sea rocked us. I closed my eyes, but that made it worse because there was nothing to distract me. I opened them again. The ship ahead grew closer. It wasn't a big ship, but I'd seen vessels that size on the Thames that had sailed in from foreign lands. It was big enough to take me far away.

I heard a splash from back near the shore.

"What was that?" the fisherman asked.

Antonio picked up the lantern. "Nothing." His face was serious though. "We're nearly there. Speed up."

The fisherman had already started rowing quicker. He turned to judge his distance when the boat tipped sideways. He shrieked. There was a scream in my throat too, but it caught halfway.

"What are you doing?" Antonio yelled.

"Nothing!" the fisherman yelled back.

"Well, do something!"

The boat lurched again, even harder. We were thrown sideways. Antonio's elbow cracked against the wood and he swore loudly. I looked up at Heaven. Maybe it was my time to die. Maybe my time had really been when I tumbled out of the wherry into the Thames. Mama shouldn't have saved me. If I'd let Griffin read my stars, he would have told me that my destiny was to drown. I'd avoided it the first time, but now it had come looking for me.

"Hands!" the fisherman shouted. "Did you see the hands?"

Antonio looked left and right. "You're mad! The only hands are yours and they're not on the oars. Row, will you!"

We were so close to the ship I could see the sailors moving around the deck. A sail had been loosened and the wind had turned it into a taut triangle on a high mast.

As the fisherman grabbed the oars, the boat listed again. This time I saw the hands before they disappeared.

"It's an octopus!" The fisherman's voice was as high as a child's. "It's going to tip us out and eat us!"

"An octopus does not have fingers." Antonio's voice quivered as he spoke.

"Then it's a dead man. He's risen from the sea to drag our souls down to Hell."

"Then he will die again."

Antonio pushed me aside, pulled the knife from his scabbard and raised it above the edge of the boat. He grinned at me. "I think we will all be meeting the devil tonight."

"The other side, you fool!" the fisherman screamed.

It was not just hands. A body rose from the water, gripping the side of the boat. Antonio thrust his knife towards it. At that moment, the boat turned over. Once more, I was sinking. My hands were tied, so I couldn't even try to push myself to the surface. Yes, I had been right. My destiny was to drown.

MAY DAY

I was flipped on to my back so my face was out of the water. Somewhere behind me, I could hear shouting and splashing, but it was getting further away. This must be the moment before I died. God was preparing me to take my soul. It wasn't so bad, rocking on the water. I let my eyelids sink down. Soon, it would be just calm water and me gliding towards Heaven.

A hand slapped my face, not hard, but the sting made my eyes snap open. My body folded into itself like an arrow shooting down towards the bottom of the harbour. My legs kicked and my head went under. My mouth was like a ladle scooping up river water. I coughed hard and felt myself sinking again.

I was hauled to the surface.

"It's me," a voice said. "Jacques Francis. Be calm or we'll both drown."

Jacques Francis? I tried to lift my head to see, but my body rolled sideways.

"Calm," he said. "Stay calm."

He tilted me so I was on my back again. I took a deep breath and tried to stretch myself across the top of the water. Above me, the sky was blurry with stars. Below me, the river was rising and falling in its own quick tide. I breathed out, slowly. I was moving. No, I was being moved.

"You're doing well," Jacques said. "Can you kick your legs a little? It will help us move faster."

I tried, but my skirt was weighing them down. The cold, the fear, the sodden wool of my clothes, it was all too heavy for me. I closed my eyes again.

"Stay awake, Eve! You're nearly there. You'll be with your mama soon."

Mama?

"I heard you singing, Eve," he said. "As you walked down French Street. I followed you and waited. I hadn't heard that song for so many years. Portuguese mothers sing it to their children when they're trying to make them sleep. Can you sing it now for me?"

Could I sing it now? My throat was rubbed dry and my tongue was a dying fish, flapping around in my mouth.

"Let me help you," he said.

He sang the first few words. His voice was rough and he had to stop to cough out water. I mouthed the words. No sound came, but I carried on, making the words come alive in my head. Soon my heels were dragging against stones and mud and I was lying still. It was as comfortable as the best bed I'd ever slept in. I let my eyes close again.

"Stand up, Eve!" he said. "We can't stay here."

Jacques Francis's voice seemed to come from a faraway place. Stand up? I just wanted to lie, slowly sinking into the mud.

"Eve! Come on!" His voice was sharp but I still couldn't move. He stooped down and lifted me up from under my shoulders. "We have to walk to stay warm."

We had come ashore by the salt marsh. Jacques Francis propped me up as I tried to stumble beside him. Night pressed the cold into my skin. I was shivering again, so hard I must have made his bones rattle too. My feet were too numb to feel for the ruts and holes beneath them. My foot jarred against the bottom of a ditch and I almost brought us both down. Jacques snapped a long stick off a bush and swept the way ahead of us.

"One more step, Eve. Just one more."

Left, right. Left, right. Just one more step. Just one.

I was sunk into a hollow of warmth with blankets tucked around me. I tried to raise my head, but my neck was tight and sore. It had been two days now, with Widow Primmer and Mama taking turns to sit by my bedside. This was the first time I'd woken up and found myself alone.

"I've made some porridge," said Widow Primmer, appearing at the doorway.

She came and sat on the chair next to my bed and held the bowl out to me. I shook my head. The thick, rough mixture would grate my tender skin.

"You have to eat."

I knew that even if I swallowed a small spoonful, I wouldn't be able to keep it in my stomach.

"Try it," she insisted. "There's half a jar of honey on it. That should help it go down."

She brought the spoon to my lips again. I opened my mouth and let her feed me. It was very sweet and my stomach seemed to like that.

"Where's Mama?" I said.

She leaned in close. I realized no sound had come out of me.

"Mama?" I tried to say again.

"Oh! Your mother! Don't worry, she's eating breakfast with Claire." Widow Primmer sighed. "I'm so sorry that she won't be able to care for Claire much longer."

I tried to push myself up, but my arms were as weak as a baby's. Widow Primmer smiled and shook her head.

"Lie down, Eve. If your mother can care for my daughter, I can care for you." She pulled the blanket back round me. "The priest at All Hallowes has recently lost one of his servants. I suggested that your mother might like to take her place. She'll receive wages and if she stays living here, I'll charge for lodging, though it will be within her means."

My mouth moved again. Widow Primmer recognized the word.

"Claire? Yes, Claire will miss her. But your mother will still see her every day. They won't be separated yet. More?"

She wiggled the spoon in front of my mouth. The porridge was so solid it didn't move.

I mouthed, "No, thank you."

Widow Primmer let the spoon thump back into the bowl.

"Well, you've eaten more than yesterday."

She stood up and took the bowl back downstairs. I forced myself to sit up. I didn't want to sleep all the time. In my dreams I was either locked in the vault with the scurrying coming closer and closer or I was in the cabin of the ship, with nothing but the sound of water around me.

Later on, I learned that the fisherman was called Luke Wolverton. He was sixteen and lived with his father and four sisters in a tumbledown house near the old friary. He'd managed to right the boat and had been heard calling for help the next morning, as he tried to paddle it back to shore with his hands. I never saw him again. I believe that he travelled to Portsmouth to work in the dockyards there.

Antonio's ship had been heading to Lisbon. It was against the law to take slaves from England, but Mama said that if he'd been caught, he could have claimed that Mama and I had run away and that he was just recovering his master's property. Widow Primmer had laughed. She'd said that she couldn't imagine Mama running away from anyone. There had been a short moment before Mama had laughed along too. If Jacques hadn't stopped them, I would have been on that ship. I thought of how hard Mama would have searched for me, running from gate to gate, from Houndwell down to the mudflats, knowing that every day her chance of seeing me again grew slimmer. Even worse for Mama, she'd have know exactly what was in store for me.

One good thing happened though: Mama and Jacques finally met. After we arrived back at the apothecary's in French Street, he'd found a set of the apothecary's wife's old clothes for me to wear. She'd died many years ago, but the apothecary still kept all her belongings. Jacques built up a fire and, after changing his own clothes, went off to fetch Mama. I was terrified about him leaving me alone. Every time the shadow of a flame flickered across a wall, I was sure it was Antonio or the fisherman, creeping round the house, ready to take me again.

It felt like I had waited all night, but Mama said that she'd left Widow Primmer's straight away – after she'd recovered from the shock of seeing Jacques Francis at the door. She had run almost the length of the town to be with me. I was taken up to sleep in the bedroom while Mama and Jacques sat on the hard wooden chairs and talked all night.

Time passed. After three days I was well enough to get out of bed and it was back to helping Widow Primmer with the chores. I had even more chores than before, now that Mama was working at All Hallowes and Widow Primmer cared for Claire. Thanks to Mama, Claire spent more time out of her chamber now and her hair was growing back. It was red like her mother's, but curlier. Claire helped me stack wood by the hearth and sometimes she'd take turns with me to churn the butter.

April came. Jacques Francis left for London. He had been waiting for a ship from the Lowlands bringing ceramic bottles. He also took with him a letter that Widow Primmer had written on Mama's behalf. I'd been in the room as they composed it. Jacques promised to deliver it by hand directly to George Symons at the Tabard.

Dear Master Symons,

I hope this letter finds you in good health.

I fulfilled our agreement and spoke to Jacques Francis. He has assured me that all the gold and other valuable cargo was taken from Southampton Water and returned to their legal owners. There is nothing there.

Master Francis will deliver this letter directly to you. If you are in any doubt, you can speak to him for confirmation.

Thank you for the pains you have taken to help me. All monies owed will be paid to you by Michaelmas.

I commit you to God's protection.

Your humble servant,
Mistress Joan Cartwright

I think Mama was sadder to see Jacques Francis leave than she wanted me to know. In the days before he left for London, he would meet Mama at All Hallowes after she'd finished working and walk with her back to Widow Primmer's. He'd sit by the fire while Mama was in Claire's chamber and when she came out they'd sit there; sometimes they would talk, sometimes they'd just sit there silently. I'd watch them from the top of the stairs and wonder if they were talking to each other without saying words aloud.

I still hadn't told Mama that it wasn't just George Symons who'd hoped to make a fortune from her. Griffin and Gina would be on their way back soon. He must have started a new bead bag by now. There was no treasure. I couldn't give him what didn't exist, but I would find work to make sure he was paid. I was good at scrubbing pans and well-practised with a sewing needle. There were almshouses in East Street and more outside the walls by St Mary's Church. Perhaps they needed help in the scullery or with washing and mending the bed linen. I would offer my services and use the money to pay off our debt to Griffin. It would take time, but there was no quick fortune for him to find.

April ended and the town prepared for May Day. Mama and Widow Primmer were to take Claire – it was the first time she'd been allowed to attend. Widow Primmer had ordered new outer gowns called kirtles for both of them, one in pale-green damask for Claire and a sky-blue one for herself. Mama had embroidered a mantle for me to wear over my shoulders to brighten my old clothes. It was made from cloth leftover from the kirtles, blue on one side and green on the other. I wore it with the green showing to celebrate the start of summer. As we came out of the house, the whole of East Street seemed to be flowing towards the square. Claire tipped her face up towards the sun as if she had never felt its warmth before. Perhaps she hadn't. Before we arrived, her world had been her chamber.

There had been a spatter of rain earlier and we had to dodge the mud and muck in the street. It looked like an army of geese had marched this way before us. Widow Primmer looped her arm through Claire's right arm, Mama through Claire's left, and they made a game of dodging round the dirt. The May Day dancing had already started in the square, weaving the ribbons flowing from the maypole in and out. Some of the dancers were very serious, while others were laughing so much they were tangling themselves up. A piper and a drummer accompanied them, though the dancers seemed to be moving to different tunes in their own heads.

Outside the church, an acrobat bent over backwards until his hands smacked on to the cobbles. He scuttled from side to side like a crab while giggling children surrounded him. He stopped by a group of young men and invited one to stand on his stomach. Just as I persuaded Mama to come over with me for a better look, a juggler threw three red clubs into the air and Claire laughed out loud.

"I think we'll be staying here," Mama said. "You go and look round then come and find us."

I walked back past the acrobat. He was still scuttling around but now he had a young man sitting on his stomach, laughing and waving a tankard of ale. In the far corner was a table bearing three big boxes. A crowd was stooping low looking into them. They were cabinets and in each one were miniature rooms, furnished like a rich man's home – if the rich man had been very small. The dresser looked so real that I was sure the doors must open. There were even tiny pots and pans in the kitchen and a shelf of bowls and plates. It looked like the craftsman had shrunk down to the size of a beetle to make them.

A drum started up. The May Queen must be on her way. Widow Primmer had said that the cart would be decorated with garlands of flowers and that the queen handed out posies as she went. I couldn't see the cart yet, but the drumming was getting louder.

"Ladies and gentlemen!" *Bang! Bang! Bang!* "It's time for the stars to foresee your luck!"

Gina? It *was* her. The white costume was a little too small now and had grown grubbier since Bartholomew Fair. I searched around for Griffin, but I didn't see him.

That was because he was right behind me. I heard his voice in my ear.

"Has our fortune been made, Eve Cartwright?"

I shook my head. I heard a sound that I knew was wooden beads knocking against each other.

"Are you keeping all the gold for yourself?"

I turned to face him. He looked even thinner than before. He was wearing midnight-blue breeches and a doublet. A dove-grey cape hung from his neck. The costume was frayed and looked like it had been pulled straight from a sack on his cart.

I said, "There is no gold, Griffin. Nothing at all."

His shoulders hunched down as he bent towards me. "I don't believe you, Eve Cartwright. We had an agreement."

"No," I said. "*You* had an agreement. You gave Mama the medicine first and then told us there was a price. You brought us to Southampton, even though you were coming this way anyway, and then told me that we were in debt. You have told me that we owe you money, but never told us the price for your services! I will pay you back, but there is no treasure."

"Hear ye! Hear ye!" The town crier strutted into the square. "Prepare for the queen!"

The crowd cheered and a piper started a tune. When I looked back, Griffin was gone.

142

We returned home soon after the May Queen was crowned. I kept peering through the crowd expecting to see Griffin appear next to Mama holding his bag of beads. He didn't. He must have been busy with his star charts. We ate supper together, Claire, Mama and I, a real feast of roast mutton and cabbage. I loved Mama, but this was how it felt to be in a real family, something bigger than the two of us. I had always known I wanted to be safe and warm at night, but I hadn't realized before that I'd wanted more than one person to care about me. Someone who could help me catch Mama if she started sinking again.

I don't remember my dreams that night. Perhaps I didn't have time to have any. A few hours later, before it was light, Widow Primmer shoved me so hard I almost fell out of bed.

TWO STONES
AND A ROPE

A candle flickered on the dresser. It was Widow Primmer. Shadows often soften a face, but her fury was stark.

"I should have listened to my neighbours!" she hissed.

"M … Mistress Primmer?"

She pushed me again. My shoulder jolted and a punch of pain shot up my neck and across my skull.

"I should never have let you stay here. You and your foul mother! I should never have agreed!"

She wrenched off the covers and I felt the rush of cold air across me. Where *was* Mama? Had Widow Primmer already wrenched her away? I touched the space beside me. I felt a hint of Mama's warmth. She couldn't have been long gone.

"Mistress Primmer, I don't understand! We have done nothing to you!"

"I trusted you." She spoke quietly, her words creating mist. Then louder, "I trusted both of you!"

Her fists clenched and I rolled into a ball waiting for the next blow. Her breath was loud and harsh, like she had exhausted herself from her exertion. The quilt dropped back down on to me.

"Get up, Eve," she said. "Pack your belongings and go."

"But I have nowhere——"

"Go to your mother in All Hallowes, though her work there won't last beyond today." She shook her head. "I should go there now to tell them. By the end of today, everyone in this town will know what your mother is and will condemn her. I'm giving you time to leave."

Claire was calling out in the next chamber. It was Mama she wanted – not hers, but mine. Widow Primmer took a deep breath and her eyes were full of tears.

"I'm sorry, Eve. You have to go."

The light disappeared and I heard her unlatch the door to Claire's room. I lay there for a moment in the darkness. There was a pale edge of light seeping through the slats in the shutter. It was later than I thought. This was my fault. I had believed last night that I was safe and that someone other than Mama cared for me. I had been greedy again. I was lucky to have Mama, I should not have wanted more. I had tried to take too much luck. I ran through my memories. Had we done anything that could have wronged Widow Primmer so badly? Yesterday at the fair, we'd been together laughing and enjoying the spectacle, the May Queen, the acrobat, the tiny rooms, the— Griffin. I'd told him there was no fortune and now we were being turned out.

I pushed away the quilt and felt for my stockings on the chair. I drew them on quickly and slipped my dress straight over my chemise. We had few belongings to pack. I shoved what little I could find in the bag I had brought with me. The new mantle Mama had stitched for me. Mama and I now had spare bonnets and aprons. A chemise Widow Primmer had no longer required and passed on to Mama.

I took one last look at our room. I had moved many times before. This was just like those times. There would be other rooms. I would make myself feel nothing.

"Get out!"

There was a shriek behind me and I froze. A wooden bowl looped over my shoulder and hit the stairs, just missing the cat that was racing past me.

Widow Primmer was standing outside Claire's room.

"Get that creature out of here!"

The cat hadn't bothered her before. There was even

a tally scratched on the wall of the buttery keeping count of the number of rats he'd caught. I felt eyes on me as I walked downstairs and over to the front door. As I opened it a crack, the cat shot out to the street. I closed the door and turned to face them.

Gina and Griffin were sitting at the same table where we'd enjoyed our supper the night before. Griffin's hand rested near the greasy smear from the custard bowl. Widow Primmer came down and sat opposite them. Her coif balanced loosely on her unpinned hair. I'd always seen her neat. I'd always known her kind. The fear was building inside me. Gina glanced away from me but Griffin held my eye. The widow must have just set the fire because it hadn't fully caught. The kindling was flaring up, shooting narrow flames towards the chimney. Griffin's face flashed dark and light. His expression said nothing.

I wanted to pull Gina away. Whatever had happened, she had no reason to be part of this. She still would not look at me. As I moved towards the table, I saw a small object. It was shaped like a woman, not small enough to live in the miniature rooms, but still not as big as a baby. As I grew closer, I saw that it had a mouth, nose, eyes, even eyebrows. It was dressed in a carefully stitched gown. I remembered sewing those stitches in the hayloft. After I'd finished the ostler's wife's sheets,

I'd repaired my poppet's kirtle, sitting by Mama's side waiting for her sadness to end. I didn't remember the poppet's hair like this, though. It was bright red, close to the colour of the strands that poked out from Widow Primmer's coif. Neither did I remember the pin that was stuck through the poppet's heart.

I looked at Gina. She was staring at the table.

Widow Primmer poked the poppet with a piece of kindling. It slid across the table towards me. "Is this your poppet, Eve?"

"Mama bought it at Bartholomew Fair," I said. "But it was not like this."

Griffin turned to me. Again, he held my gaze. "You travelled with this ... thing ... from London."

"Yes, but..."

"It's as I recounted, Widow Primmer. The plan was made in London."

I shook my head. "There's no plan!"

"So you deny it?" Widow Primmer said. "You didn't make a plan with that sailor cousin of mine to come and seek me out?"

"Yes," I said. "He said that if we helped care for Claire, you would help us with lodgings."

Griffin nodded. "As I told you, Mistress."

Widow Primmer nodded back, then looked at me. "I'm sure your mother knows that witchcraft doesn't work from afar. You had to come nearer. Did George Symons suggest that too? Use my own daughter against me to win my trust? Then render me so sickly that I'm a prisoner in my own home?"

"Mama is not a witch! We were happy here!"

"But it is not your own home." It was hard to hear Griffin's voice above the crack of the sparking wood. "You told my sister that you would do anything to have your own home."

"Yes, but…"

Griffin turned his gaze on Widow Primmer. Like me, she was unable to look away from him.

"Her mother was sick with melancholy, or so we believed. Now I understand that it was part of the bewitchment to bring them here and deliver them to your home. They were in such a hurry to set their plans in motion that this poppet was left in my cart. It was wrapped in a linen shroud with the pin through its heart." He turned to Gina. Her face was set like she was trying not to cry. "My sister found it, but has only just revealed it to me. If I had known earlier, I could have saved you more distress. But it isn't too late!"

He swiped up the doll and threw it into the fire. Its hair flared first, a ball of flame. The gown and rag body smouldered then ignited. The round wooden head smoked but didn't burn. Griffin picked up the poker and pushed the remains of my poppet deep into the fire.

Griffin hooked the poker back on to its nail. "Now it can hurt no one."

"Go, Eve. Leave this house now," said Widow Primmer.

I wanted to hold Griffin's gaze in the same way he had held mine, but I would not let him see how close I was to tears.

"The charge is untrue. I gave Gina the doll. It was a present," I said.

I thought Gina was about to speak, but Griffin put his hand on her shoulder. The fabric of her dress crinkled from the tightness of his grip.

"The accusation is witchcraft, Widow Primmer," he said. "I expressed my concerns to the beadle last night. He said he would attend to it this morning. I had to remind him that torture by witchcraft is a hanging offence. He cannot be lenient."

Widow Primmer shook her head.

"No. I don't think… I am well. There's no need."

Griffin stood up and leaned over the table.

"Have you ever knowingly given lodgings to a witch, Widow Primmer? Have you knowingly allowed this to happen within your house?"

Widow Primmer's mouth worked. A finger stabbed into my thigh. It was Gina. Her eyes were pink and sore, her face paler than the morning light.

She mouthed, "Go."

I gathered my skirts and ran. It was not far to the rector's house at All Hallowes, but it felt like I was running the wrong way round town. When I got there, the door was open and a bucket of slops was being emptied on to the path outside. It was the rector's wife.

"Where's Mama?" I gasped.

The rector's wife gave me a sour look. "How do I know? Do you think I want to do servants' work? Perhaps that sailor man turned her head."

"Sailor man?"

"The one who came here two nights ago."

Jacques Francis had returned?

The rector's wife stood upright, stretching out her back.

"I didn't mind the other one, coming to walk her home. This one, though... I don't like loud voices on my doorstep."

I touched my skin. "Was he like me?"

She shook her head. "No. He was a tall fellow with too much beard. Though I couldn't help hearing a little of their conversation." She scratched her head. "He was shouting so loud I couldn't not hear it. He was weaving her a yarn about treasure in the water and she was saying there wasn't any. I had to ask my husband to send him away. Perhaps your mother followed him later."

"She was home last night," I said.

"Well, she isn't here this morning."

She tapped the bucket so the last drips splashed on to the street and closed the door. The next time she opened it, it would be to the beadle.

Mama hadn't mentioned meeting George Symons. But then, I hadn't mentioned Griffin and the wooden beads to her. We'd both angered people looking to make their fortunes from us and we'd both kept secrets from each other. George Symons must have snatched her on her way to work. Perhaps he'd had a knife like Antonio, forcing her through the common land and orchards out towards the dock. He would make Mama dive. The Thames was treacherous but its currents were our everyday life. Mama knew nothing about the depths here. Would her nose bleed and her eyes burn? Would she become trapped between the bones of men who had drowned? Was she already struggling, her breath running out and the sea pressing around her? I stopped walking so abruptly that a man behind me slammed into my back. He swore and walked on, looking back at me, angry. I could not help Mama by myself. I couldn't do anything. I couldn't even walk.

"Eve!" Gina was puffing towards me, tears running down her face. "I'm so sorry! I'm so sorry!"

153

I wanted to be furious, but this wasn't her fault.

"Mama's not at the church," I said.

"I know," she gasped. "A black man just came looking for her at Widow Primmer's. He said it was urgent."

"A black man?"

"Yes! He said there was a man coming from London, an angry man, who thought your mama had taken his fortune."

"George Symons?"

"Yes, that was his name."

"And the … the black man? Did he say where he was going?"

"To the quay. The west side."

I bobbed forward and kissed Gina's forehead. "Thank you!"

I reached deep inside myself for more breath and I ran. I turned in to St Michael's Square. The maypole was still standing, its drooping ribbons brushing the dirty cobble stones. My feet slipped on the petals and flower heads as I raced towards the West Gate.

The quay was usually busy, but there were only a few fishermen around now. Most of them must have been sleeping off the May Day celebrations. A few vessels bobbed in the water, small boats that looked worn from travel. I recognized Jacques Francis immediately, looking out across the water. He turned round and pointed.

"They're there," he said.

I squinted. I could just see a dark smudge out on the water.

"Are you sure?" I asked.

He nodded. "We have to go to her."

"On a boat?" Just watching the gulls glide across the water made my stomach hurt. "I can't. I can't go on a boat again."

"I think he told your Mama that you'd be hurt if she didn't follow him." He crouched down next to me. "If you come with me, she'll see that's not so."

I knew that I had already drawn more than my fair share of luck. I knew that I had avoided my destiny twice already. I would not avoid it for a third time. Yet, if I stayed here, it would be Mama who would fulfil my destiny instead of me.

"I won't let anything happen to you," he said.

I couldn't tell him that if it was my destiny to drown, he wouldn't be able to prevent it.

"Stay here a moment."

I watched him walk to the end of the pier, look from side to side, then wave. A rowing boat came in to sight. It was a little bigger than the one the fisherman and Antonio had used, but still no bigger than a Thames wherry. Jacques beckoned me over. The pilot looked at me and said nothing. He was a broad-faced man with skin rubbed by harsh winds. Jacques Francis handed him a purse. The coins clinked as the pilot took it and laid it by his feet in the boat.

"This is Samuel Hambleton. He'll take us there."

Jacques took my hand and walked me to the edge of the pier. The boat rocked in front of me. My legs weren't my legs, they were part of the river, flowing away from me.

"You have strength inside you, Eve," Jacques said. "Just take one small step. Then another. If you must, close your eyes and I will help you aboard."

I closed my eyes. He passed my hand to Samuel Hambleton. I felt the callouses and roughness of his skin as he gripped me.

"Hold her steady," Jacques Francis said. I wasn't sure if he meant me or the boat. I didn't open my eyes. The fear was building inside me and I wanted to pull away and run as fast as I could, through the Bargate and on the road back to London. If I opened my eyes, I would do just that. Jacques Francis took my other hand. I stood there, my foot raised, halfway between land and water.

"Just one step," he said, gently. "One step."

I took the step. The boat moved, but the hands held

me steady. My heart was trying to beat itself out of my body. I made my other foot follow.

"The bench is behind you," Jacques Francis said. "Sit down."

My knees were wobbly, so I let myself sink.

"Well done, Eve. I'm coming aboard now."

The boat moved again and sunk lower into the water.

"Let's go," Jacques Francis said.

I opened my eyes. He had taken up the second oar. I stared straight ahead as I was propelled out and away from the land.

The smudge became sharper. It was definitely a boat. How many people were on it? One? Two? Was it really them? Closer and closer. I saw a bow, a mast, the back of a man. The man turned and saw us. It was George Symons. Where was Mama? I leaned over and tried to look down into the water. Instantly, my stomach churned and my eyes blurred. I sat upright so quickly the boat rocked. George Symons didn't move. He seemed to be waiting for us. As we drew up next to him, I saw two heavy stones in the bottom of his boat. They were tied to either end of a length of rope.

"Where's Joan?" Jacques Francis shouted.

George Symons shrugged. "I told her to bring me my fortune. If she didn't, there would be no daughter to return to."

Jacques Francis looked down at me. "Her daughter's here."

"Your infidel friend doesn't know that."

I heard Jacques Francis take a deep breath. "How long has she been down there?"

"I don't have a timepiece to measure." His voice was calm, like it didn't matter if my mother was dead or not.

"There is no gold," Jacques Francis said. "Just the poor souls who couldn't be buried on the land. I told you so in London."

George Symons shook his head. "Do you expect me to believe your godless lies?"

Jacques Francis said nothing. He removed his cap and his cape. "I will find your mother, Eve."

The water stirred by the bow. Fingers, a whole hand, a face pushed through to the surface. My mother gasped and opened her eyes. She saw me.

"Eve?"

Jacques Francis held out an oar. "Take this, madam!"

"Do you have anything?" George Symons shouted. "Have you found the gold?"

Mama swam grasped the oar and, shuffling one hand over the other, pulled herself towards us.

"Eve," she said. "I'm so happy—"

I heard the rasp of the rope and the thump as a stone hit the side of the boat.

"No!" Jacques Francis yelled.

He was too late. George Symons had dropped the rope across Mama's left shoulder. Mama clung to the oar. I reached out my hand to her.

"Mama! I'm here!"

Jacques Francis heaved the oar closer. Mama's fingers touched mine just as George Symons picked up the second stone.

"Take this!" Jacques Francis handed me the oar. It was heavy and I grasped it with both hands, but Mama's weight made the wet wood start to slip through my palms. Jacques Francis tried to reach across and grasp the other boat. Both boats swayed as he lunged towards George Symons. George Symons glanced back at him then leaned over to drop the second stone over Mama.

"No!" Jacques Francis tried to pull George Symons away. "You'll kill her!"

"Then she'll die."

The stone's weight made him lurch forward. He was still, then I blinked and heard the splash as he fell in.

"Mama!"

The rope pressed against her throat and her mouth gaped open like she was gasping for breath. Then she was dragged backwards into the depths.

The water was my destiny, I knew it. I'd nearly

drowned twice but had been saved. Did I wait for it to claim me a third time or did I run towards my fate? Did I let Mama die or did I do everything I could to save her? She was down there. She was alive. I breathed in slowly and slipped over the edge of the boat into the water.

The water isn't claiming me, I'm letting myself sink.

The water isn't claiming me, I'm letting myself sink.

As I sank, I kept my breath inside me, then I opened my eyes. The water was murky and streaked with weeds and pecks of mud. It was like the river understood that it could no longer take me. The deeper I sank, the harder it tried to push me out. I didn't look down. I knew there was a great depth of water below me. My chest could hold in the air no longer and I let myself be pushed upwards. I broke the surface and fought to stop myself breathing out in one big gasp. If I did, it would feel like I'd never catch my breath again. Instead, I blew out slowly until I was empty and took another big breath.

I looked across the water. The rowing boats were further away than I expected. What if I could never swim back to them? I pushed that thought away. I had to find my mother. I took another breath and a hand grabbed my ankle and yanked me down. As I screamed, my mouth filled with water. I saw hair floating in the tide, a mouth with a string of bubbles floating upwards, eyes wide with terror. George Symons. He was drowning and he was taking me with him.

I kicked at his hand and felt my heel connect with his knuckles. He let go and I managed to rise until my head was out of the water. I coughed and spat, my arms flailing around me. The river was fighting back. It had come for me again. A hand held my shoulders. I tried to wriggle free.

"Stay calm, Eve." It was Jacques Francis. "I'll take you back to the boat."

"They're both in the water," I said. "George Symons and Mama."

"I can't save both. Let me take you back and then I'll find your mother."

"No," I said. "No one must drown."

"But you—"

"I saw George Symons. If he's there, bring him up and I'll help him."

"I'll try once. That's all the time we have."

I nodded, rolled on to my back and waited. Mama was under the water, under the stones. I had to roll that thought up, push it away. I must only think thoughts that would let me keep floating. A moment later, one head surfaced and then another, eyes closed, wet hair stuck to his skin.

"He's alive," Jacques Francis said. "Here! Over here!" He raised his hand and waved it towards the boats. "Take him quickly, but if he drags you under..."

If he dragged me under, I was to let go.

George Symons was floating on top of the water. His eyes were closed and his mouth was open. I grabbed the shirt beneath his shoulder and kicked my legs gently.

"I have to go," Jacques Francis said. "Promise me, Eve. If he starts to drag you under, save yourself."

Jacques Francis disappeared. All I had to do was to keep George Symons afloat until the boat came. My arms were already hurting. Should I be here with this man who didn't care if my mother died? Perhaps I should let him go. I had jumped in to save Mama, not him. My fingers loosened on the back of his shirt. I turned a little to look at his face. Nearly thirty years ago, he hadn't been much older than me when he was cast into the sea and knew that his uncle was dying below him. It hadn't been his destiny to drown then and it wouldn't be today.

I heard the swish of oars in the water and lifted my head. The rowing boat was close. Samuel manoeuvred towards me. The oars clunked as he dropped them on to the bottom of the boat. He leaned over and grabbed George Symons' shoulders, grunting hard. The boat tipped but didn't capsize.

"Lift his legs," Samuel said. "But take this first."

He handed me a pale ball, an inflated pig's bladder. Some of the wherrymen carried them, especially those who worked close to the bridge and worried about capsizing at high tide. I held the bladder in my hands and hooked my arms around George Symons' legs and heaved up. I only moved him a few inches, but it was enough for Samuel to pull him the rest of the way into the boat. George Symons landed with a thud.

"I have to take him back to shore," Samuel said. "Are you coming?"

I shook my head. "Not yet."

Samuel nodded. "I hope God's luck is with you all."

He rowed away. I let myself float on my stomach, face down peering into the gloomy water until I had to lift my head for a breath. How long could Mama hold *her* breath? No one could for this long. Down there, there were masts and anchors and bones and maybe even treasure. The river had secrets and intended to hold on to them. *Please don't hold on to my mother.*

I heard my name. It sounded far away. I saw an arm waving in the air close to the shore. That was Jacques Francis. Where was Mama? I kicked my legs hard, holding the bladder with one hand and pushing through the water with the other. The water became shallow and my feet kicked mud. I stood up and waded through, my feet sticking in the troughs left from the waves. Mama was there, lying on the shore. Jacques Francis was crouched over her. As I ran towards her, I saw her face was covered in blood.

I dropped down next to her.

"Is she alive?"

He looked at me and said nothing.

AFTERWARDS

Jacques Francis isn't angry any more. He told me that he was angry when he jumped off the boat. He was angry as he plummeted towards the river bed. The water there was so deep, he said, because two rivers met by the quay. That was how his anger felt, surging towards him, whichever way he turned and without end. The same way Mama would sink into her melancholia, he would sink into his anger. Eventually, Mama would surface from her sadness, but he was never free. He felt the buzz of his anger every moment of the day.

If it wasn't for me, he would have let George Symons drown, especially if losing him meant saving Mama. Jacques had learnt many times that all lives were not equal. His own, he had believed, was worthless. He would save Mama. He would save me. Everybody else could die.

As the water closed over him, his anger had softened. The weight of the water crushed it from him. On land, he felt the ache in his knees when he walked and in his wrists when he gripped a horse's reins. In the water, he was twenty years old again. His body was light and moved without effort. He had opened his eyes and it was like visiting a land that he had once known well.

"Except there were no boats beneath us. The big ships anchored further out. It was deep, but I had been deeper."

He had felt the familiar ache in his ears and behind his eyes. He had pinched his nose and pushed his tongue up against the roof of his mouth. He hadn't even thought about it, he did it instinctively. Down he went and that's when he'd seen Mama. She had shifted the rope from her throat to her chest, but the stones were stuck in the mud. Her arms and legs were floating above her, her eyes were closed. He had lifted the rope; there was little slack. As his chest ached, he'd managed to shift one of the stones enough to free her. He knew they were surfacing too quickly, but there was no choice.

George Symons survived. His younger sister still lived in Portsmouth and he was taken there to recover. I do not know what became of Gina and Griffin. Now I am in Southwark again, I think that one day I'll turn a corner and see them, especially if there's a fair. When I hear a drum beating I expect to see a small girl in a white costume, but like me, she'll be nearly fifteen now.

166

I miss Mama, but I'm grown and should make my own life. That's what she tells me when I visit her on Sunday afternoons, though she's always happy to see me. I care for a surgeon's children, helping his wife with the baby and four others while he's at sea. It will be at least a year before he returns. Since Francis Drake came back with his riches, every merchant wants to sail to the other side of the world to find gold or rob a Spaniard.

Jacques Francis is still an assistant to the apothecary, though the apothecary is rarely behind the counter these days. His eyesight is so bad he can't see the labels any more, and he almost poisoned a mercer's sister two months ago. Now Mama and Jacques are married, they both live above the shop too. They haven't found any medicine that can cure Mama's deafness, though it is not as bad as two years ago. Even a month after her rescue, she couldn't hear anything and the pain deep inside her ear made her cry.

On Sundays after church, we walk along Bankside and watch the ships as they sail out towards the sea beyond. I think Mama and Jacques sometimes talk of returning to the countries where they were born. They know, though, that everything has changed. They weren't the only ones who were stolen. What if they return to find their friends and family were also stolen into slavery? What if they're captured again themselves? Mama still believes that we must trust no one. She trusts Jacques Francis, though. I can see it in her eyes. And Jacques? Yes, he cares for Mama too. But when he stares towards the sea, there is another expression on his face. He's the man who would, for one last time, like to jump from the rocks into the sea and swim to shore with an oyster in each hand.

"Come away from the water, *mpendwa*."

I don't know if Mama is talking to me or Jacques, but he takes her hand and they turn away from the river.

AUTHOR'S NOTE

I grew up in West Sussex in the 1970s and 80s. I have two very strong memories from that time that influenced this book. Firstly, a homework assignment when I was about nine. We had to imagine ourselves as a character from Elizabethan times and write a story. I loved history and I loved writing stories even more. However, I struggled. I think I even cried. As far as I knew, people who looked like me were not in England in Elizabethan times. My mum put me straight on that. She said there were people referred to as "blackamoors" around, even then. I started writing my story with renewed vigour.

A second strong memory is the raising of Henry VIII's flagship, *Mary Rose*, from the bed of Portsmouth Harbour in 1982. It was like a ship from my imagination coming to life. However, like most of the British history I had learned about, I felt at a slight distance from it. Every history lesson I had absorbed, every book I had read and picture I had pored over as a child, every UK-set historical film and TV series I had ever sat through, told me that people who looked like me had no role in British history other than being slaves.

Now, I know better, of course. Peter Fryer's *Staying Power: The History of Black People in Britain* was an eye-opener! I had no idea that black people had been part of British life for the last two thousand years. Many years after reading that book from cover to cover, I was researching the history of black people around the City of London and Hackney. The Institute of Historical Research has a list of church entries starting in 1573 – baptisms, marriages, burials – of people with roots in Africa and Asia. I cannot help but wonder about all those lives, many of them servants, some skilled workers, some of them living and dying in poverty. My heart bleeds for the nameless man who was buried on 29 June 1588 in the churchyard of St Olave's on Hart Street, City of London, after being found dead in the street.

I had bought Miranda Kaufmann's *Black Tudors: The Untold Story* a few weeks before I was asked to write this story. A happy coincidence! I was attracted to the story of the diver, Jacques Francis, because the raising of the *Mary Rose* was a significant moment in my generation's history – and also, it wasn't too far from where I grew up. There is also the enduring myth that black people can't swim. What the story of Jacques Francis showed was that sometimes, black people were the only people who *could* swim! Jacques is also one of the first recorded Africans to give evidence in an English court. It's a really significant moment, but lost – or trivialised – in the history books.

However, I wanted to tell the story through a child's point of view. I did not want to focus on slavery, but I also knew that people from the African continent were being kidnapped and exploited by European countries such as Portugal and Italy for hundreds of years. In 1570, when my story is set, slavery was still considered illegal on English soil. Though it did not mean that people of African descent were safe.